HEADGAME

To Lorraine
Thanks for your support
B

beesusnshyne@yahoo.com
Copyright © 2010

®

Production Coordinated by GOD
Edited by R. Little
Cover Design: Bill Macadam

HEADGAME   by Brandy

Head Game © 2010 by Brandy. Manufactured in the United States of America. All rights are reserved. No part of this book may be reproduced in any form or by any electronic or mechanical means, including photocopying, recording, or by an information storage and retrieval system except by a reviewer who may quote brief passages in review to be printed in a magazine, newspaper, or on a website without permission in writing from the publisher. For information in writing from the publisher, please contact @ rsl@alittlepubications.com

ISBN 13: 978-1-949720-89-1

This book is dedicated to my Uncle Bubbie, Grandma Jessie and Grandma Heglar you will be missed and may you rest in peace. I would to thank my Kids Ashan and Delvon Jr for supporting me. The staff at ALittle Publications and my editor R. Little for inspiring me. I would to thank my mother Vanessa Leocadio and father Stanley "Biggie"Hegler. A shout out to my Brotha Stan jr and Sista Nicole "Mama" . Know this shout out for all my homegirls: Syreeta and Sharon Ocala Massive, Sister In laws, Nicole,Crystal, Marlowe, and Kyatra, Zakira, Tasha (ATL), Yaa (BRKLN), ATTISE u know who u r, Renee, Tara, Cassandra, Reeree, Shavonda, My

HEADGAME   *by Brandy*

supporters out on 60th Street, Debbie, Ngozi, Sheryl, Tawonda, Annette, Crystal, Darnetta, Jade, Margi, Jedda, Keesha, Latiesha,Latoya, Michelle, Niccee, Shante,Shawn, Sonjee,Trina, Lois, Joy, Sophia, Buff, Tasha, Nicky, Kenya, Sandra W, Cali. Danni, Ebony, Alia, Vanessa, Phil, Robert Little, Uncle Tyrone, Aunt Jeannie, Mae, Gianna, Erica, Catina, Nayah, Tajuana, Lashonta, My CCP Peeps, Patreice, Tanika, Patricia, Chris, Mike, Michelle,Johnett,Antoinette,Ms Debbie, if you don't see your name then fill it in right here_____.

To all my Hustla's
Black and Nobel Hakim, Tyson, Akil, Gus, Norman, Joesph Church Keep ur head up, Philly Bookman, Empire Books, Zahir, Tiffany. JoJo from StreetKnowledge Books, Derrick King, Xanyell, Leroy

A note from the author

I was inspired to write this book after going through my own trails and tribulations. Vickey was inspired by my life experiences. Headgame is not all about using and selling your body. It is about making the right the choices and decisions to get ahead in this life. I choose this title because to survive in this life one must have a strong and positive game. This is for all my ladies that are in the struggle and can

HEADGAME *by Brandy*
identify with Vickey. To all the haters and the back stabbers. God Bless You!

Hit me up on facebook and myspace!

beesunshyne@yahoo.com

HEADGAME　　　　　　　　　　*by Brandy*

"Where there's a will there's a way"

Coming into this world I didn't have anything but a shitty diaper on my ass but that didn't stop me from turning shit into sugar. If you ain't got riches or bling than you ain't shit and no one loves a broke ass fool. Just take one look around and you will see these niggas rollin in Benz's, Escalade's and Beamer's gettin all the love. Don't forget about the iced out bracelets with matching rings. They are a must have in this baller society we live in. I know ya'll be seein em showin off. The baddest hood bitches and flyest model chick wearin the tightest gear. BET gets me especially excited, watching the hottest videos and all that I truly desire are plastered on the screen; money jewels and power. I love the flashiness and the way it demands respect.

I'm thirsty to have it all and a chick like me is gonna have it no matter what it takes or what I have to do. I've been grindin since I can remember. Shit! I've been hustler since the day I was born. I'm from a small tribe called "get-ta-monee" and I am the war chief. I grew up in the slums of West Philly right off of Belmont and Girard Avenue y'all might have heard of it. To be honest with you it's a pure shit hole. My rotted building reeks of piss and shit. The dope fiends often scratch, node and threw up

HEADGAME by Brandy

at my front door. However I fantasize about having my own place out in the country. The green pastures surrounded the land as I lived in a large million dollar mansion.

The kids in my class claimed that they wanted to be policeman, fireman and doctors. I dreamed of bein that hustlin chick with minks, furs and cash to burn. I would visualize me holding and counting stacks of money everyday. On the days I didn't have a dime to my name I cut up pieces of paper like it was money and stuck it in my pocket. I'd wrap aluminum foil around my fingers as if they where the latest bling. I was determined to get the riches even if it was none in sight. I can remember my first hustle like it was yesterday. I would pinch off my Dads weed stash and sell it to my class mates for a profit. After I did that for six months I accumulated over a thousand dollars in cash. My dad was one of the largest drug dealers in West Philly, his reputation was fierce and no one dared to play him. But since his death eight months ago my life has been spiraling out of control.

I was Daddy's little girl and he spoiled me rotten since I was his only child. Our relationship was something special and he cared for me unconditionally. In his eyes I could do nothing wrong and I missed the way he hugged me tight. I was his little princess and he was my king whom I loved so dearly. Daddy was always telling me about how nigga's is after one thing and I needed to make sure I was with the right guy. I wasn't allowed to have a boyfriend until I was in my early teens. If word got around that I was seeing

HEADGAME   by Brandy

someone he would ease up on the seen and interrogate dude. He tried to protect me from those monsters that were out to prey on me. Sometimes I hated when he preached to me about being a good girl and how I should be patient about who I trust. I wondered did he ever take heed to his own advice because it was his close friend that set him up.

He was shot and killed while sitting in his car, some said he was robbed but other say it was an execution. I didn't know who to believe but if I ever found out who killed him I would kill them. Just thinking about him made me mad and filled with rage.

Daddy met mommy at the Thanksgiving party at Temple University and since then they have been inseparable. They were married soon after I was born and the rest was history. They laughed at each others corny jokes and stayed up all times of night listening to oldies. My mother tried to be strong and hold herself together but when he died he took a piece of her. She was never the same after that and slowly lost touch with reality. Mommy was crushed with the lost of Daddy and took it harder than anyone expected. I thought our love and bond would pull us through but I was mistaken. She was so consumed with grief that the drugs and alcohol became he comforter.

The times where getting hard for me and my mom with the lights cutt off and facing eviction. My mom once the Queen of the ghetto is reduced to a common crack whore. My Dad supported her crack habit but know he wasn't around she turned to

HEADGAME   by Brandy

trickin. Her "friends" as she calls her Johns come around all times of day and night. I can hear them moaning and groaning - up all night. The smell of cigarettes and cocaine was engrained into the wall. My mother stop taking care of herself. Her teeth quickly rotted and she smelled of old moldy pussy. Her fine wavy hair became coarse and matted. She wondered the streets and spoke in rants.

After my seventeenth birthday and years of dealing with my mother addiction she lost her mind and was committed to an insane asylum. I was alone in this world and I only had myself to depend on. I tried to go out on the block to sell weed but those vultures harassed me every chance they got. Without Dads connection and protection I got robbed for my package. At gun point I was not told to not to come back around on the block or else.

It was hard trying to make a living with no skills and basically nothing to offer anyone. The girls that I knew were trying to have babies by the big time drug dealers so they could have a free ride. I liked the free ride part but that baby shit was a no-no. I was sure that I did not want to have no table pimps, rug rats or little greedy as kids tagging along with me. I barely could take care of myself and imagine the strife I'd have to go through life with a kid.

I dug in my pocket and looked through my cabinets. All I had was peanut butter and ten cents. I ate the last of the roman noodles yesterday and wished for a steak. On some occasion I would go over to my girl friends house or the Chinese

HEADGAME *by Brandy*

restaurant down the street to eat. My pockets were empty as I looked for spare change. I wished my mother was here because she would now what to do. She always had a scam or hustle to get some money. It was then that I was realizing why my mother made the hard choices she made. As my stomach growled with hunger I became more understanding and less judgmental of my mother's past acts.

She did the best she could with what she had. I remember she'd sit my down and explain to me about life hard lessons. You have to give a little to get a little. I was willing to give all I had for the small comforts of being taken care of and not having to fend for myself. I didn't have anyone to give my all too and I surely didn't trust my broke ass of a boyfriend, Roger.

Roger and I are childhood sweethearts that lived on the same block since we were knee high. He was short and stocky with the long beard. He calls himself a Muslim but I hardly ever seen him pray and he still be eatin ham sandwiches. He goes by the name of Talib now. We haven't been that much of a couple lately because he wants me to take my shahada and wear a full grab. I like eaten pork chops, wearin my tights jeans and heels. He wasn't gonna control me and I wasn't gonna let him. I told him that if you want to be a Muslim than go ahead but I'm not into it. Since that conversation he's been comin around less and less. He hasn't called me in a week and I'm fine with those arrangements.

HEADGAME   by Brandy

In the bottoms we had to code of silence like must hoods. If they thought you to be a snitch or a rat your days were numbered. I rolled with the punches for awhile but I was slowly starving. I tried to find a job but I had no such luck. So what's mother fucker to do. Then to top this shit off this fat mcnasty ass landlord is bangin on my door.

"Good evenin, Ms. Vickey I'm here for rent. You do have the rent?" I didn't now what to tell him because I had nothing to give him.

"ummm I don't have it," as I tried bash my hazel eyes at him. He salivated when he spoke and straight throw me.

"I have been nice and I let yah stay here but I need my money but if don't have cash there is other was to pay", as he moved closer grasping my small waist. The smell of his breath on my face made me sick. The throw up push past my stomach and stuck in my throat as I wiggled free from his grasp.

"*Ill have your money in two weeks. I promise you,"* I begged giving my best performance.

"*I don't now,*"

"Please, Please, Please" letting a tear fall down my cheek. I was always able cry at a drop of a dime. It got me out of trouble and I hoped this time it wouldn't fail me. I peeked out the corner of my eye to see if I was getting to him.

HEADGAME   by Brandy

"OK I'll give you fourteen days and if you don't have my money then its curtains for your fine ass." as his fat smelly ass turned away and walked out the door.

SHIT! Look at this roach infested hole in the wall. The plaster was pealing and the holes in the windows are covered with plastic. The mice ran all over the apartment. They chewed holes threw the walls and left shit around here. How am I gonna get this nigga's money?

I'm stuck like chuck and facing eviction. I really needed a plan to get that rent up. Truthfully I wanted to trade my pussy for rent but I couldn't bring myself to do it at least not with him. I wrecked my brain tryin to squirm out of this mess and all I could come up with is that I needed me a victim that to suck and fuck into submission. The only problem was I never sucked a dick in my life. I could do anything when my mind was made up.

It ate my up inside thinkin about all my options and from what it look like I ain't got to many. I know what I said about pride and not bein able to trick but what am I gonna do know. I'm not tryin to live in no shelter nor am I tryin to be homeless.

I decided to pawn the only thing I owned of value in this world and that was my mother's gold pendant. It hurt my heart to even think that I would have do such a thing. I promised her that I would hold on to it because it was the only thing she had that was owned by her grandmother. I knew many of times she was ready to sell it but resisted the

HEADGAME   by Brandy

temptation. I was on my way to the pawn shop on Lancaster Ave. In my mind this was priceless and should be able to get a fair price. I was hesitating about going there because I heard several different stories of how they ripped people off. The outside of the building looked as if it was out of the seventies movies. The high yellow paint screamed out to the neighborhood that it was here but it still was a horrid sight. I inched my way to the gated booth where the young men sat anxiously awaiting break time.

"Hi,"

I passed the pendant through the bars and waited for his reply.

"Yo here for loan or pawn,"

"Pawn" I noticed his manicured fingers, lip-gloss and eye shadow he applied to his face. He was a handsome young man. I might of given him some if he wasn't so feminine.

He twisted his mouth and finally announced his offer.

"Giveya $25"

"That all, this is a family treasure"

"You can take it or leave it,"

"OK"

HEADGAME   *by Brandy*

He filled out the forms and asked for my ID. I signed my name; they took a photographed and a finger print. I held the money in my hand and walked out the door. I placed the roll of small bills inside my purse. I didn't know that i was being followed by the neighborhood dope fiend. I walked down the block not paying attention when I felt a hard tugged that knock me to the ground. I sprain my leg as I rolled under a car. I looked at the fiend as he run away with all the money I owned. I cried as I limped back to my apartment. I was ruined and helpless with no other options. What would my mother do? It was time for me to grow up and face this cruel world. It's either eat or be eaten alive, a lesson I learned dearly. From now on I vow to slay anybody that gets in my way. I refuse to be poor and struggling again. I will stack the cards in my favor.

" Where there is a will there is a way"

HEADGAME   *by Brandy*

The Headologist

I was not graced with wealthy parents nor did I receive a trust fund. Poverty was the vain of my existence and seemed to be all around me. The abandon buildings stood in a row as garbage parked on the front of buildings. The Korean store owners littered the avenues as they plotted on the black dollar. The suffering in my hood was great and we all fall victim to the grips as it pulled us all in. If you wanted get out the ghetto and spring from its ashes one must be willing to do all she has. Not just ready to cry and speak of its hold on you but to fight this temptation to give in. I had no skill or a prince fuckin charmin to rescue my black ass. I had to make it the best way I knew how and have to use all that God gave me, lip, hips and finger tips. I decided that I would use my body to get what I really needed in this life. Some like to call it

HEADGAME by Brandy

whoring, tricking and prostituting but I just call it surviving. I'm not gonna sit around and fool myself on what I was resulting to. Being moral and upright seemed to be killing me as the streets were sucking the life outta me. It has taken my hope and faith, so now I must live as they live and become a savage beast. I had a plan and to me it was a very good one. I wasn't gonna stand on some corner wave at passersby or straight trade pussy for money. I was not that bold and I be damned if I was gonna let some fool ass niggas jump up and down on me.

I needed a single victim one that would sponsor me out of this ghetto. The credentials I was looking for was large pockets and a kind heart. I've known girls that get involved with some real guerilla type dude. They like slapping bitches or using them for a punching bag. That was the one thing that I wasn't havin my ass gettin kicked by some guy. I didn't like guys with a whole lot of baby mamas and children all around the country. I understood one or two kids but a whole basketball team thing was out of the question. He needed to be rich and looks where a third on my list. I figured if I could succeed in getting two outta three then that would be just fine with me.

My ex-boyfriend Roger was my first and only sexual partner. When we had sex it was mainly him on top humping like a jack rabbit for a good 10 or 15 minutes. He'd been finish business just before I got warmed. I be like damn, *you finish already.* However, he would lick on my clit and let me cum in his mouth. Ooh!, I liked the way he did

HEADGAME *by Brandy*

that to me. His dick was lacking but his head game was excellent. He would suck my pussy dry and I was hypnotized by his tongue. I was stuck in gear with Roger's shit and I needed to be free from his grasp. Fuck, em let his little bitch-ass suck somebody else's pussy.

My sexual experience was limited and I wouldn't know what to do when it came time to get down to it. My fuck game was nil and my head game was none existent. To me I thought that suckin dick was veil and disgusting. I wondered how women could do it and drank cum afterward. It was beyond me to think that I could ever learn to do such things. There are tons of bitches out there tryin to get ahead of the game doin cartwheels and flippin over shit to get t a nigga's pockets. I wasn't goin to be freak of the hood but I would catch me one guy who can take all this loving at one time. I would give him all my treasures and in return he would give me the world. I would not be defeated on this one nor would I take any prisoners. Love and security was mine to be had and I was goin to have it by either hell or high water. So my new twist would be to tighten up my headgame.

I didn't know the first thing about given head and was really scared when confronted with the real thing. I needed to change my outlook and be the bitch with flyest head game in the city. My new persona needed not only to suck a dick but it was a part of the whole movement I was starting. I needed to change everything about me from the inside to the outside. I needed to be sharper then the rest and willing to take all the chances that

HEADGAME   *by Brandy*

none of those other bitches are willing to take. A real animal I wanted to become, to live off of instinct rather feelings and emotions. The mind set changed from prey to predator and I was no longer goin to be anybody's feast. Momma's gonna prepare the food and serve these nigga for dinner.

First, I needed someone to teach me how to change my persona to that gutta chick that specializes in eatin a dick. My goals were to blow minds one at a time. Once I got on a nigga's dick his fuckin toes curl and make him holla like a little bitch. I was ready to fuck a nigga dry and if his pockets are fat enough he could have it all.

All this plottin and planin is wearing my out. The beginning of my plan starts with finding a true mentor and confident. I kept tryin think of a female that could teach me. I thought of my aunt Pam but that snobbish bitch never sucked a dick in her life. She'd have all my business in the streets and probably would have to kick her ass with that smart ass mouth of hers. I required a thorough ass bitch who wouldn't think twice about gettin her knees dirty but played the game well. I needed a Headologist not some amateurish bitch that's gonna play games but a bonafide gag and spit bitch. I searched my mind and flash,

"CARMEN!" I yelled.

Carmen is my play mother and confidant I knew since I was a kid. She practically raised me and when my mother was in the middle of her battles she would leave me with her. Carmen was the

HEADGAME by Brandy

closet thing that resembles family and she would do anything in her power to help. Persuading her to give me her know how was going to easy but I would have to bare my soul. I have to tell her the tryin times I facing. She's lived in the hood so long that nobody bothered nor disrespected her. Carmen has a lot of skills from cooking up coke and dope to running card games in her house. Her claim to fame was her legendary head game - she is a bonafide headologist.

Back in the day I used to see "tricks" come to see her for favors. She wore minks and drove the hottest rides in the city. Her jewelry was from the finest stores as she worked over players for their hard earned cash. Pimps never tried to lean on her or make her choose because of her no-nonsense style matched with a razor she carried. Of all the people I knew she was the one that can get my head game to the professional level. I needed to persuade her to teach me. Carmen never took nobody under her wing and didn't like females in her business. To make ends meet drug dealer paid her to cook up their dope. I never asked her for her help and this would be the first time. I was desperate and I would have to make it convincing.

On the next day I walked over to 27th and Girard to visit Carmen. She lived in a well kept and moderately furnished row house. When I arrived she was already sitting on her swing on top the porch sippin a glass of that , "yak". Her faced was round and hard, while her eyes displayed the hardships of life. A silk robe wrapped around her thin figure with her long legs crossed. Her long

HEADGAME   by Brandy

fingers where holding the burning Newport 100. She sat there as a loved and revered queen exhaling a long stream of smoke. Most people called her Ms. Carmen but I was one of the few who called her momma.

"HI MOMMA!, " excitedly waving my hands to at her.

"Who dat iz!," She quickly responded while squinting her eyes, without her bifocals she blind as a bat.

"It's me momma, Vickey"

"Ahh dats my baby, "Pooke Dooke "She shouted. She's been callin me that since I was baby and hated it then just like I hated it now. We gravitated toward each other and embraced warmly.

"Come on baby sit next to momma" She remarked warmly. I was shy and I couldn't just come out and say what was on my mind. At first I mumbled some words and talked some other bullshit.

"Girl, I know you ain't come all the way to talk some bullshit, so come spit it out,"

" Iya...... needed you to help me,"

"Helpya like what?"

"Ok, Ok, I need you to teach me"

"teachya what"

HEADGAME *by Brandy*

"You know.... the game, howta play niggas"

"The game is to be told not sold, what are willing to give,"

"Give? All I have is me to offer,"

"Exactly what you need to give...is you and it ain't no turnin back, once I giveya what I got"

"Ill do anything say"

"You bet your sweetass you are,"

"Damn Pooke areya sure your ready for this cause this here is make ya or break ya," her apparent concern appeared over her face.

"You got to understand either I start makin it do what it do or I'm gonna be homeless bitch and I be damned if I'm goin to the shelter "

"I'm the last one to judge you but if you gonna be down, you gotta be cold as ice willing to do all that i ask"

"So are your gonna help me , PLEASE, PLEASE, PLEASE" I begged and squeezed her hand.

"Aight pooke dooke but u gonna do things my way, I'll show you how to play a nigga and how to turn him into your bitch. Imma show you the ropes but you betta use your skills wisely." Carmen replied as she displayed her tobacco charred teeth.

HEADGAME   by Brandy

Damn! I wish I knew what I was gettin into. She started by making me do jaw strengthening exercises. I stretch my mouth into kisses, then in O's and twisted them to side to side. I did the mouth stretching drills for hours until my face got numb. Then she had me doing tongue exercises - sticking out my tongue left to right. For the past three days I worked hard at my strengthening exercises. I practiced every time I got a chance and even out in public where niggas thought I was crazy. I exercised my lips and tongue everywhere I went. I needed to build up my muscles in my jaw, so I did what I was told.

I worked my jaw muscles feverishly as I repeated several phrases, "me me me me, pe pe pe pe , te te te," over and over again. I held cucumbers in my mouth for as long as I could. As days went on I was able hold it in my mouth longer. I held it between my jaws while steady inching it down my throat. I rolled the cucumber around my mouth while fighting off my gag reflexes. I got so good that I could go an entire hour without getting numb. Carmen was proud of me and said I am the fast learner.

"You've built up your muscles well but now you must work on your technique, some bitches like to do a little hand jerkin but I don't" She stated as she pulled out a 12 inch dildo. She placed a condom over it and swallowed the thing without gagging. I put a condom over the banana and mimic her every move. I slid the it in and out of my mouth. I circulated around the tip, rolling it and swallowing the other half of it.

HEADGAME   *by Brandy*

The other part of her training was learning how to entice a man. She grabbed the large mirror and showed me how I slouched. She insisted that I stand straight. I also practiced using a soft tone and charm when I talked. I practice sizing men up by looking at their shoes, clothes and watches. I recognized a fake ass player as soon as he approaches. I evaluated a nigga within 30 seconds and became quite good at it. When Carmen finished with me my head was exploding with knowledge and my head game was tight. She armed me with the best weapon she could, a strong mind and the know how to get what I want.

 A few days later that landlord showed at my door. I hadn't a dime to my name and I had to make up my mind fast. By the time I answered the door he was breathing hard and gasping. I stripped down to my bra and panties exposing my thick shape. When I opened the door his eyes popped out his head as I stood there. His fats ass limped inside and stood behind the door.

"DAMN! You fine" he managed to bark

"Is this worthya rent?" as I unfastened my bra straps and covering tits with other hand.

"It could be," he sharply replied

"I need more time in my apartment?" while lowering my arm and exposing the brown of my nipples. I know what I said earlier but a bitch is fucked up right now and I ain't got to much pride. I'll write this one off as an experiment. I quickly

HEADGAME   by Brandy

dropped to my knees and unzipped his fly. I reached inside to find his small size penis. I closed my eyes and imagine it was Chris Brown standing in front of me. I licked around the head and his dick grew to the total of four inches. I moved up and down shaft while rolling my tongue. I deep throated it but when it felt like it was extremely hard I stopped.

"Please don't stop, please" as he tried push my head around his dick.

"I need more time," as I rubbed the head of his penis with my thumb

"OK, OK take as much time as you like, just finish," he begged like little a bitch. As soon as he agreed I jumped on that dick. I stroke it with my entire jaw and brought him into a full climax. He squealed as I took his entire load into my mouth.

"OH FUCK! OH FUCK!"

"Now get the fuck outta of my house," as I wiped the corners of my mouth. I pushed him toward the door and motioned for him to leave.

"But I Ummm."

He tried to say something but I didn't care to hear it. I continued nudge him closer to the door before he could realize what was happening.

I lay across the couch and laughed my ass off when he finally stopped bangin on the door. I

HEADGAME   *by Brandy*

couldn't get that silly ass sounds he was makin out my head. I needed to find me a real nigga cause I can't be doin him for a long time.

HEADGAME *by Brandy*

Hello Beautiful

I didn't say this was gonna be pretty and nor was it going to be easy. I didn't mean to get down with the landlord and after I said I wasn't gonna do it. What's done is done , but its a new day and bitches out here don't give a fuck about you. They ain't thinkin about me, bitches around here rather seeya fucked up , walkin around talkin that luck shit. There ain't no luck or miracles, you gotta make your own luck. I gotta do what it takes to win and win I must. So don't go around judgin me because only God can judge me.

The second lesson Carmen taught me was sometimes you gotta lose to win. You can't always meet force with force, you may have to let the bigger man defeat you so you can mount your attack and that's just what I was doin. I'm crazy but I'm not stupid my motives appeared to be free rent ,but my true purpose was getting a hold of that money filled wallet the landlord is carrying around. The stack of money in his wallet is what I needed

HEADGAME   by Brandy

and I was gonna have it. That's why I pushed him out the door before he could get his shit together. He probably so proud that he got his dick sucked by the young gal. It was like I hit his ass over the head while he wasn't looking and I bet he ain't gonna tell his wife.

I've been picking pockets since I was a kid. I learned that for my moms when things got really bad for us we'd go down to Center City and catch us some victims. The game worked best when she bumped into them and I would reach for the marks' wallets. I got real good at it after my first couple of tries, my moms called me a natural. In school I would steal lunch money, pens and whatever I could get my hands on. It came natural to me and beside dramatically crying at the drop of dime that's what I was good at.

I watched my mom hustle her ass off , "*Mimi* " as she liked to be called flipped dollars while doin all kinds of shit. She wasn't always trickin for crack, her most favorite scam was credit card fraud. She'd get stolen credit cards from a crooked postal employee who was jonesing for crack. He'd steal bundles of cards and bring them over to the house. In return for the cards he would receive small amounts of crack. I was amazed as the bags of stuff travel in and out the apartment. Our house looked like Grand Central Station as people came around selling every thing from prescription pills, weed, dope, pussy, blank checks and food stamps. My mom very rarely hid anything she did, she was a regular gansta bitch who loved the money and finer things in life. Her jewelry sparkled and I could

HEADGAME   by Brandy

always hear her walking. The bangles wrap around her arm jiggled together making that funny clicking noise. Even today when I hear bangles rumbling I think of her.

While she did her dirt I was right there as her witness. Sometimes I was partner and at times an unwilling participant. I learned that being frightened and scared don't pay. My mom was liked to a lioness in the wild and we were her pride. She didn't play that stealin shit or runnin off with her money. I've seen her kick many bitches' asses for that disrespectful shit. I can remember mommy thought Daddy was steppin out on her and how it caused such a big scene. She headed right over to the lady's house knocked on the door and when she answered all hell broke lose. She snatched the lady out the house and tore her nightgown off and started punchin her in the face. Word got around fast that if you messed with MIMI's man you got a problem. After that I never heard anything about my Dad and another woman. She tried to school me to scams and how to get a mark. I didn't understand what she was doin at that time but now I realize her teaching me how to survive. How to eat and not be eatin I'd like to think. Mimi didn't allow you to run away when the goin got tough. As a kid I got picked on by the biggest girl in the school. I ran home crying and frightened. When Mommy found out about that she marched my ass outside and told me if I didn't kick her ass, she was gonna kick mine. I straightened up fast and charged that big bitch. I knocked her to the ground and begun beat the shit out of her. I learned a valuable lesson that you must be bold and move

HEADGAME   by Brandy

with confidence while doing your dirt. "It's all in the mind," she used to say. I believed I could whop her ass and I did.

I lifted the landlord's wallet for a total of five hundred dollars cash and some credit cards. I needed some new clothes and I didn't want to let these credits card go to waste. Its only right that I take myself shopping because my current wardrobe was faded and dingy. Even the ten dollar store shit I was rockin was to small with the stitches ripping. I had four main outfits that I mixed and match. My shoe game is wanting and needing a facelift. I'd clean my sneakers so much that the bleach piled off the white paint. A chick like me needed an upgrade and for what I'm planning I betta come correct.

I never let my clothes game fall off like this. My Mom would pay the booster for my clothes and since my mother was away I seemed not to be able to muster up the courage to strike out on my own. It was easier for me to do things when she around because her confidence radiated from her. I knew that thing would be just fine if she told me so. I remember that glare in her eyes and with times I would have that glare of confidence. I needed to draw on that energy after all I am my mother's child. I inhaled and closed my eyes picturing me walking into the stores and pulling clothes off the racks and charging his cards. I imagine myself trying on its latest fashion and engaging the sales staff as if Id been there a 100 times.

HEADGAME   by Brandy

I searched my closet for something to wear. I didn't have anything because they were cheap and worn. I decided to search my moms closet even though she was a sizes smaller. I was determined to find something to wear. I dug to the bottom and I found a picture album with pictures from my childhood. I stopped to look through the pictures and there was couple from a Halloween party when I was young girl. Mommy made me dress up like a princess. I had scepter, crown and large shear dress. I remember that day like it was yesterday. It was the first time I remember seeing father lose his temper. It was at that party I remember watching my father beat the shit out his friend for stealing money. He throw him over kitchen the table and smashed his head into the concrete wall. He pulled his gun and was ready to fire until he realized that I was standing there. He holstered his weapon and told him that it was his lucky day. I never saw my father that way again but when mommy found out he pulled a gun in front she lost it.

I turned the pages and recognized the pictures of our last Christmas together we were so happy then. The abundant smiles on our face give no hint that in a matter of a couple of months that we would be split up and on separate paths. I discontinued looking at the pictures and slammed the book closed. I threw it across the room watching it bounce of the wall. I hated it and wished I could burn it because all those memories made me sad. I looked through the closet and the

HEADGAME by Brandy

two piece skirt hanging in plastic was perfect. I pulled my hair back and noticed that a lump of hair falling out. My hair was a disasters as I truly needed my ends cut. I managed to put in a bob with a ponytail in the back. Shit, after I'm done shopping Imma go get my hair done. I applied make up and lipstick to grant me the illusion of being older. The heels were a seven, a half size smaller than I wore but I was able to stuff them on my feet. The results where acceptable and I was ready to make a move. I pushed the if's out my mind and focused on the mission at hand. No matter what I was coming back with new shit.

That afternoon I rode on the trolley and landed on Market Street with its busy afternoon traffic. The cars were rumbling up and down Broad Street as they followed the road signs. I walked straight to Macy's department store with the must determined look in my eyes. I was ready to growl because I was full of ambition and dared anyone to stop me. I never bought anything for Macy's and only came here to steal with mommy. I entered the corridor the smell of newness permeated the air and I loved that smell. I was psyched as I pulled the clothing from the racks. While entering the dressing room I hoarded many of the dresses. The fitting room was filled with clothing that I deemed un fit for me. I made conversation with the other consumers and had the sales lady looking after me as if I was royalty. I didn't stay in one department; I toured the building stopping to see whatever peeked my interest. I visited all five floors and wondered into

HEADGAME   by Brandy

the employees lounging area. I rode the elevators as if I was posing for the camera.

I brought several pairs of designer jeans all tight fitting; ; Apple Bottoms, Guess, Baby Phat. While I tried on the clothes, I felt like a million bucks. I loved the way my round breast fit inside my new dresses. The jeans exaggerated my curves and hugged my firm plump ass. I bought blouses, skirts, shirt, stockings, lingerie, bras and Victoria secret panties. I surrounded my feet with snake skin boost, Kenneth Coles and Nine West.

The sales lady showed me all the latest designs and was glad to assist in charging his credit card. When I showed the platinum card, she quickly informed that I had no credit limit. I nearly fall out my seat at the thought that I was spending all this money. She folded my clothing in the bag and neatly stacked them by the register. The total came up to $3447.40 and I didn't even blink hard as I handed her the Platinum. I watched as she slid the card throw the machine, it felt like time paused for the 30 seconds. The register begun to rattle as it started to spit out the receipt while "Approve" flashed on its screen. I scribbled my name on the paper and slowly dragged the bags toward the door.

I decided to spend some cash on a much needed manicure and pedicure. I desired a French

HEADGAME by Brandy

manicure because I loved the way they looked on the models in the fashion magazines. I sat in the middle chair while getting my feet down. I laid my head back and eavesdropped on the conversations the girls next to me are having. I chimed in on their sexual exploits and looked as they showed off their bling. I envied them for their ability to get over but that shit they were talkin was overboard. I laughed when they ridiculed dick sizes and tales of the niggas that can't fuck. My loud laugh alerted them to my spying but since I had all those bags sitting on the side of me, I got a pass.

After I got a French manicure and pedicure the only thing left is to get my hair dipped. I've since tried to do my own hair but with no luck. I've worn my hair in a ponytail for so long that I forgot how I look with it down. The back was cut shoulder length while the front was cut in a short bob. I inherited my long wavy hair for my mother. My hair ends where split and the leftover dye give me an odd look. The stylist dyed my hair jet black and cut off the ends. I looked like the Egyptian Queen Nefertiti when she finished.

It was the end of the day and I was exhausted. It was very dark out side and I dare not take El train home with all these bags. My hand was unable grasp all those bags. I was able to get this far because of the adrenaline pumping in my veins. I waited on the corner until the rickety old cab recognized its future patron. The cabby spoke little English with a strong accent and I was force to be

HEADGAME   by Brandy

patient with giving him directions. During my ride home I fell back into my seat and said goodbye to the old me. I realized in the past twenty four hours, I tricked, robbed the landlord and committed fraud at a major department store. I caught the reflection from the window and I saw my mothers glare in my eyes. I was my mother's child and I would take on her traits. I ignored the consequences of my actions and never would I again hesitate to gamble big. I knew I was destined for something great but I just couldn't figure it out. All I knew was that I was victorious today and I promised myself that I will keep on winning.

I finally arrived home and it was already 10pm. I opened the door and that familiar little mouse I've been tryin catch ran for cover. I dropped the bags at the foot of the door, pushed the light switch and illuminated the room. I looked around the small living room and everything was exactly as I left it including the now crumpled photo album. I ran to pick it up and I soon regretted throwing it. I brushed it off, straightened out the pages and sat it back in the closet. This was all I had left of my family but it takes a good minute until I travel that path again. I lay on the couch and fell asleep within 10 minutes.

The next day I look at all the bags strayed all over the apartment. I cleaned them and lay out my new outfit. The answering machine was blinking and alerting me that I had a messages awaiting so I pressed the button

HEADGAME   *by Brandy*

"dis iz Carmen, pickup da damn fone fool, I got somebody I want you to meet tomorrow, he'll be over here bout 11am so have yo ass here by 10:30 am, Don't be late!"

She hangs up the phone and I was already late. I hurried to the shower and when I finished I unwrap my hair. I stood in front mirror wearing my tight guess jeans, halter top and black stilettos. I combed out my wrap letting my hair flow down to my back. I placed the gold hoops on my ears and sprayed some White Diamond perfume all over my body. I smelled and looked good. I couldn't believe what a make over could do for me. I turned to the mirror and for the first time in a long while I looked myself in the eyes.

"Hello beautiful!"

HEADGAME *by Brandy*

Victim

The new clothes and hairstyle help my confidence and I was no longer feeling sorry for myself. I was prepared for the meeting at Carmen's house and whomever she had in front of me was in for big surprise. I knew she had something big in stored for me. I had been preparing to meet a real big player but she never mentioned his name to me. After my begging her to tell me who it is was unsuccessful I just left her alone. My anxiety was high and the anticipation was killing me. All I knew was that it was one of the ballers she cooked up for. I would have to leave if somebody showed up for business. I was instructed not to say a word unless I was spoken too and had to keep that to a minimum. She implied that in the ballers circles you just can't all of a sudden show up in the business. They need to see you around or they might suspect you're an agent. By me hangin with Carmen I was gaining credibility with out ever sayin a word. Eventually I was allowed to work on some occasion. I started packaging dope with Carmen and that paid $500 dollars a sitting. I ran into few players from the hood but I didn't pay them any attention. I was happy that she was helping me and confident that I was ready to move on to the next stage of the game. I searched my mind of who she wanted me to meet. She warned if I got

HEADGAME   by Brandy

involved with the wrong payer things could go bad very quick. Once your claimed by a baller your off limits to the rest and all other prospects have to wait. If your not careful you can be kidnapped, rapped or killed.

I often wondered if I was ready for the life and what it had in stored for me. I opened my mind to all the prospects good and bad. I truly didn't understand what I was getting into and didn't hesitate to kicked the doors open for the fast life. I was bred for it and only needed a kick in my ass to get it jump started. I seen what one good player good do for you and I needed to have it. One day you could be eatin oodles of noodles and the next you could eatin lobster and skrimps. I was tired of living in my world of emptiness, settling for the scraps and leftovers.

I hated my dainty dark apartment and I wished I could move outta there like yesterday. It was cramped with memories and the walls seemed to have a voice of its own. I'd lived in this apartment so long that I would even know how to get out. It was all that I had and I'd ever known. The old place had such an escapable hold me that I even dreamed of it. I didn't know why I felt like this or maybe it's because I had nowhere else to go. I wished for some family that would take me in but my fake ass family be trippin. When my father died it became obvious what type of vultures they really where. While we where at the funeral somebody mysteriously broke in and robbed us. I got a feelin in the pit of my stomach that it was them. Since my mom departure I haven't seen their cruddy assess.

HEADGAME   by Brandy

They either eatin up my stuff or askin to borrow money. The closest relative was my younger cousin Charles "Money" Diamond and he's doin a three to seven in Gratersford PA super max. Charles was like the big brother I never had. He got locked around the same time my Dad was killed. I ain't ever been to jail and I don't plan on going anytime soon.

I applied my finishing touches and glanced in the mirror looking for anything that was out of place. I twirled around then I struck pose to reveal my new found sexiness. I closed the door to that my apartment and begun my walk toward Carmen's house. I confidently swayed my hips and strutted like the thorough chick that I am. The confusion started when my plump ass attracted a lot of attention. The guys in the street seemed to lose their freakin minds as I made my way. The parade of horns beeping at me made me nervous. Even Poppy from the corner store took notice of me and why he shouldn't.

"Holla Mommy," he squealed as he searched my body with his eyes. I grinned with approval and walked with that "come fuck me twitch". I stopped at the corner and painted on my black cherry lip gloss giving me that I just ate a dick effect. Oh, Don't get it wrong I'm no ugly duckling but it's a rare occasion that I dressed up and let my hair down. I was what you called a diamond in the rough. I had nothing to loose and everything to gain. I now understood what the rapper Fifty Cent meant when he said get rich or die tryin. I wasn't

HEADGAME   by Brandy

rappin to no beat but I was gonna play to my own drum.

My travels through the hood brought me a lot of attention. It was over bearing but I just took it all in. The cars that pulled to the side, I just wave them off. I'm no street hooker or whore - that's not my twist. I was looking to be loyal and for someone to help me get me out of that fuckin dungeon. I was lookin for is a sponsor, lover and friend. I thought about how some chicks get caught up hookin and turned out by drugs. I promised myself that I wouldn't go that far. I seen what that life did to my mom and watching her slowly die was horrible. The first couple of times she did it she was okay but as time went she needed more drugs to hide her pain. She didn't mean to turn out that way but time was against her as she slowly fall into her rut. I didn't want that lifestyle for me and vowed I would kill myself before I let myself go.

By the time I arrived on Carmen's block I got two marriage proposals and followed by some creep in a Navigator. He waited on the corner until I passed. He licked his tongue and winked his eye at me. He honked his horn several times but I ignored these gestures for my attention. He was creepy old man and I didn't want to get kidnapped by some crazy pervert. I screwed my face up and clinched my hand bag ready to pull my razor. This was my moms old rusty razor that I carried for good luck. She warned that some people might what to scare me and make me ugly. She showed my how to take it out swiflty and the best way to slash somebody. I kept walkin and nigga's kept tryin

HEADGAME   by Brandy

holla at me. I was already late for my very important date. I hoped Carmen would forgive me but knowing her she was not gonna have any excuses. I hoped that once she gotta look at me all will be forgiven. I rise above worry because I know that I was making an important entrance and I wasn't goin to be denied. My confidence was shaky but I was ready for whatever.

In the back of mind I am still tryin get over suckin off the landlord. Shit I've been tryin to put that one in the closet and avoid ever speaking about it again. If it ever comes back to haunt me I will deny just like the rest of you bitches out there. Imma write that one off for the team but it did pay off in the end. I aint homeless and I got somewhere sleep at night. I seen nigga's gettin they shit thrown out on the curve. Everything they owned gets piled on the sidewalk while the neighbors stare at you. All your worldly possession gone and when it gets dark the dope feinds start picking through it. So my choices where far and few as I wiped my forehead as I broke out inna sweat as I thought about chosing the landlord's dick instead of homeless bitch. Okay I'm done and I ain't gona tell that story again but I admit that shit was nasty. Hell ,"sometimes you gotta move backwards to move forward" that's what my momma used to say.

I finally landed on Carmen block and it was quiet. I walked down the street and as I got closer to her house a brand new black BMW was parked out front. It had chromed rims and tinted windows with a custom paint job. I couldn't resist touching the sparkling car. When I leaned against it the alarm

HEADGAME by Brandy

sounded, "intruder *approaching car back up, intruder approaching car back up"* I was embarrassed that I set off the security system. The car sounded loudly and immediately a familiar face glances out the window. I moved gracefully up the steps being careful not to trip. I daydreamed about owning that most beautiful car I'd ever seen. I pictured me driving the car up Market Street and sitting in its leather interior. It was a pretty car and only a true baller could afford it. It made me very curious about who was sitting inside the house. I kept track of all the ballers cars in the hood but Id never saw this one before. I had some low level ballers tryin to get with me but I wasn't havin it. I was determined not to date the help. I was boss material and I carried it that way. I believed that I owed it to myself to acquire that best life had to offer.

Carmen was sitting at the table with a mound of white powder and the sexiest ass nigga I seen in my life. He looked like Idris Alba and with one glance he made my pussy pop. It seemed like time slowed as he raised his thick eyebrows while looking at me.

"Damn Carmen, Who dis? He asked he leaped from his chair.

"I'm Vickey ," I interrupted Carmen because she might of say my name is "Pooke Dooke". Oh, I hate that name and being first impressions are ever lasting I wanted ensure mine started off good.

HEADGAME   by Brandy

"Vickey! Is that you! I HARDLY Recognized you dressed like that, Its Omar, we went to jr high" as he wet his juicy lips and extended his hand toward me.

"Omar is that you!," as I smiled

Omar and I grew up on the same block and climbed trees together. I hardly remembered he was in my class and back in the day he looked like a young Steve Erkel. We embraced for a moment letting him feel how grown I've had gotten.

"Wow Vickey you changed so much," he added as he gave me that look like he was ready to fuck me right there. I looked like Polly Anna with my long pigtails when I was younger. I was skinny and flat chested but since then I've blossomed. I can tell by the way he looked me at that he was giving me his undivided attention.

He didn't know it yet but he was going to be my first victim. I grabbed his hands giving a pleasant squeeze ensuring my finger ran up his palm. My eyes invited him to continue watching me but I still wasn't sure if he was feelin me. Carmen checked out what was happening and didn't bother to say anything. She continued to mix the heroin while tasting some on it on the tip of her tongue. She scooped and weighed the concoction as if she was a chemist. I always thought of her as an old pro that was out to pasture but to my surprise Carmen is one of the most sought after dope cutters in the game. Her mixing ability brought in clientele from

HEADGAME   by Brandy

all over. She'd mix the heroin so good that all the dealers from Philly paid her a visit.

I heard about Omar and that he was on his way up the ranks. The word on the street was that he inherited an entire block from his father a member in the Philly Cartel. One of the ruthless drugs gangs known around the "city of brotherly love". I didn't knew how paid he was but I guessed he was worth a couple millions of dollars. I wanted to be a part of that team so I decided to get in where I fit in.

"Damn Shorty you need to let me take you out. What do you like to do ? He asked leaning his body toward mine.

"I love cheese steaks; you can take me for the best cheese steaks in Philly"

Omar and I hit it off from the start. He was a strong type guy that could give you an answer with just one look. His eyes were cold and dark as if he expected to kick the world's ass. He'd sit and watch my every move as if he was painting a picture of me. Some times his stares made me nervous because I never had anyone look at me so intensely.

Our first date he decided to go to Atlantic City. We slept in separate rooms and had fun talking and walking along the boardwalk. We watched the aging soulful singer from Philly perform her classic hits from the 70's. It was the most magical night that I ever had. We had so much in common and

HEADGAME   *by Brandy*

since then we started spending more time together. Within two weeks I was practically living with him. Omar insisted I be with him all the time. He brought me a small car even though I didn't now how to drive. I was moving toward,"wifey" status. I was pulled into his world facing all the excitement and dangers it had to offer.

HEADGAME   by Brandy

Met at the Cross Roads

Carmen guided me every step of the way and soon recognized that we where comin at a cross road. We spent a lot of time together and I was falling for Omar fast. He was everything I was lookin for and much more. It was like I knew him from my past life and I couldn't fathom goin on without him. I was really getting used to bein around him.

Only after a month of seeing each other Omar made it clear that he wanted me for himself and demanded I will live with him.

"Vickey I love you and I need you by my side. I see how you are faithful to me and I love that about you. So, We goin to pick up your stuff tomorrow"

"Is that ya way of askin me to move in,"

"I didn't askya nothin, this what your gonna do,"

I knew he wanted to be my protector and care for me. Since the month we been together I have been home only to change my clothes. I mostly stayed at his house. His home was designed beautifully

HEADGAME   by Brandy

compared to mine. His wall showed murals and the floor had wall to wall carpeting. It had all a nigga needed, Flat screen TV's in every room, a king size bed with the softest' superpedic mattress. Every time I lay on it I was in a deep coma. The painting of African art was enlightening but I liked the poster of rap artist placed on the wall. On the warm summer day he turned on the central air conditioning and froze me out. When I was living at the old apartment I was lucky to have a cheap ass fan circulating the hottest air. It made an awful noise as it buzzed, clamored and rattled. I thougI ran into garage and climbed into the Range Rover.ht the blade was gonna fly off and kill me. I didn't want to seem ghetto but I ain't never felt central air. I was so hype because I was finally movin on up!

Moving in with Omar was a financially good move because that meant I would no longer have to worry about being taking care of. I talked a thousands of times of how I wanted to leave my old riggety apartment but as the opportunity arises I was scared to leave. This meant that I had to now depend on him. I wondered if he would he put me out in the streets if things didn't go right. My fear was genuine and understandable but it was time to move on. I was in that hole for to long and it was time to break free of that bullshit.

Omar could sense the doubt as I wanted to get out of our deal. I really felt confused.

"Are you sure you want me here, "

HEADGAME   by Brandy

"Ain't no women of mine, gonna be stayin in some shit hole like that, people be talkin and if you gonna rep me that its got to be all the way,"

"What happens if you don't want me anymore? Are you gonna throw me out to the streets,"

"I'd never do that shit to you and besides if anything ever happens I'll make sure yout taken care of, trust me okay"

"OK"

I decided that I would put some trust into Omar. I was ready to move in within a couple weeks but he insisted that I get my stuff today. I hugged him tightly showing how much I appreciated him. I thought of how much stuff I was gonna take. He must have heard what I was thinking.

"You don't have to bring no furniture with you all you need is your personal belongings I'll send a truck for the rest of the stuff"

I was careful to shake my clothes out when I go to my apartment for fear that one of those roaches might hitch a ride. Them cockroaches from my house don't die they just multiply. I tried spray, bomb, chalk, acid and a preacher's sermon but they still survive. Now I had the task of clearing draws of my stuff. I decided that all I needed was my new clothes and my photo album. Everything else I would gladly give up.

"Do you want me to help move?"

HEADGAME by Brandy

"I can do it by myself and plus I need sometime to think,"

"That's my Vickey always wanna do it by herself."

"I gotta do this my way, I've gotta say my goodbyes in my own way

"Aight Just call me when you finish"

"See that's why I love you

"Oh you love me"

"Yes, I do"

"I love you too Vickey,"

This was the first time we ever mentioned love to each other and I believed our pledge. I held him close as my emotions were ragging with joy. I really found love for the first time and I was goin to be happy.

When I arrived outside my apartment the landlord was kindly waiting on the steps. His face lit up like a light bulb as he watches me walking toward him. I was wearing my cut off shorts exposing my toned legs and the fatness of my ass. I can tell by the looks in his eyes what he wanted and what he expected from me. However, he is in for a rude awakening and I was ready to give to him. He rubbed on my ass as I passed him to go the apartment. I avoided talking to him as he followed me up the steps with his face damn near in my ass. He was so closed to me that I could smell his breath.

"Hi Ms. Vickey, Howya doin today?" He asked while holding his hat in his hand. He looked like a stupid ass school boy and I can tell he's still open from our last encounter. I rolled my eyes and switch my fine ass right to the lock door ensuring he geta good look at my ass cheeks. I knew he is here for his rent and I wanna make sure he gets everything he came for. While he stood at the door looking like a starved wolf. I was fiddling with my keys trying to open the doors

"You know your special to me Ms Vickey and I never wanna cause you any trouble but I need a thousands dollar rent, " He smiled.

"A THOUSAND DOLLARS!," I yelled out and folded my arms.

"A thousand dollars or some of that sweet head you given with a little pussy on the side," He stated tugging at my arm.

"GET DA FUCK OFF ME,"

"Don't be actin like that,"

"I said get the fuck off me, I ain't given you shit, yah fat bastard

"Oh now you wanna act like that,"

"I ain't actin like nothin,"

HEADGAME *by Brandy*

"Since I bought those fine clothes you got in that closet, I deserve some of that pussy"

"You ain't buy me shit!"

"I know it's you, that stole my credit cards and wallet, I found the receipts on the floor"

"You have been in my apartment!"

"My apartment! So either your gonna give me some of that pussy or I'm gonna call the police"

"I ain't steal shit,"

"Listen hear you little bitch either you suckin some dick or goin to jail," he yelled. He grabbed me by the arm while forcing himself into the apartment. I ran to the living room and he chased behind me. He grabbed the back of my collar and yanked. He ripped my brand new shirt. I turned quickly knocking his arm away and kicking for the family jewels. My first kick missed but the second was dead on target. After my foot impacted the large man withered over. I aimed the mace on my keychain at his eyes and began to spray. I aint never heard a grown man squeal that loud. Ya'll shoulda seen this fat mutha fucka hit the floor. He was rolling around screaming in pain.

"Oh you think you can just come over here and take advantage of a bitch huh,"

HEADGAME   *by Brandy*

I planted the tip of my sneaker to his face. I was more ferious over my new designer tee shirt he ripped.

"I didn't mean it, I didn't mean it," he begged as he tried to cover from the beating he was receiving. I snapped with anger and hit him with what ever my hand touched. "Crash!" My moms favorite vase over the head. "SMASH!" The Chair sounded as it broke into pieces.

"That's for makin a bitch, stoop low"

"I'm sorry,"

"You was gonna try and take the pussy, you wasn't even goin try to bribe a bitch,"

I continued to punish him and beat him with no remorse. When I finally finished the entire kitchen was lying over this mother fuckers body. He just laid there with out movin. I thought I might have killed his ass. He finally sat up and lay against the wall. When I finished packing and I walked toward him.

"No No No more," He yelled.

"I bet you think twice about fuckin wit a nigga next time,"

I removed his keys off my key ring and threw it at him. The first key missed but the second key bounced off the side of his head.

HEADGAME by Brandy
"There is your rent,"

I wiped my brow with my forearm. It felt good to get even because payback is a mutha fucka. I dragged what I needed to the curb and called Omar. He soon picked me up and noticed that I was sweaty.

"What happened to you?"

"Ah just tired from pulling these bags, take me home,"

Omar and I where officially living together and everything seemed to be going well with our relationship. He took good care of me and i never wanted for nothing. We moved into a house out in Chester County, that's the suburbs right out side Philly. The home was huge and I didn't know what to do with all this space. In the garage we parked our cars. He bought me a Range Rover and he drove a BMW. The Range Rove I got for my birthday. I didn't know how to drive when he got it for me. He taught how to drive and eventually I was able to travel on my own. I picked up money and spent hours counting it. We had about seven shoeboxes filled with cash.

He was a member of Philly's Cartel his family belonged to this gang since the early fifties. His father was a founding member and the current leader. Omars duties were go to meet his heroin connection. He never divulged me with a lot of information because it could gotten us in a lot of trouble me. All I knew is when he returned from his

HEADGAME   *by Brandy*

trips he had a large brief case full of heroin and Carmen mixed it with the cut.

He showed me his stash of weapons and money. He suggested that I learned how to shot. I didn't like the deafening sounds that guns made. I was truly scared of them but I started to learn the smaller caliber like the 22's, 25's and 32's. I didn't like shooting but Omar said I needed to know how for just in case. I was falling in love with Omar but I wasn't about to kill no one.

Omar needed to understand that I was not going to be some cowgirl. There were guns in every room and I was familiar with all the hiding spots. He kept a gun inside duffel bag full of cash in the garage. The emergency cash of a hundred thousand dollars was inside a basement inside an old oil tank. A get-away car was parked across the street. If anything should happen to him. I was to grab the money, car and drive to his parents house. A few times I contemplated about taking off with the cash but I was scared that he would find me and kill me. Omar was no sucker and would bust a nigga's ass in a heartbeat.

After I picked him up at the Amtrak Station we went home and made love like we hadn't seen each other in years. As I was riding his dick the intruder alarms sounded. Omar sprung out of bed and knocked me to the ground. He ran to the closet and pulled out the sawed off shotgun and two nine millimeter pistol.

HEADGAME   by Brandy

"Get dress," he yelled as he put on his sweat suit pants. I grabbed my robe and begun to shake. I was never this scared in my life. He stood by the door while I hid under the bed.

"What the fuck is goin on?" I asked him. He just starred at me with a blank look on his face. He put his ear to the wall and his finger to his mouth signaling me to be quiet. Before, I could get out my reaction. TATATATATATATA! Bullets came through the door and knocking it open. Omar shot back and each time he fired my body jumped.

"FUCK!" I screamed as I balled into the a knot praying I don't get hit. TATTATATATATAATTA sounded the machine guns as the bullets came flying and puncturing the sheet rock. Omar jumped over the bed and covered me with his body.

"Aight baby we got to get out of here. We gonna go out the window and climb down." Omar commanded.

"On three go," When he counted to three he begun to shoot. BOOM! The shotgun sounded as the pellets filled the air. He dropped the shotgun and aimed the two 9mm down the hall. BLOCKA! BLOCKA! BLOCKA!. Meanwhile I fumbled with the window and dove on to the ledge. I crawled to the edge of the roof and jumped to ground. When I looked behind me I didn't see anyone. I did as he instructed me to do incase of an emergency. I pulled out the driveway and Omar was standing by the window with one leg hanging down.

HEADGAME by Brandy
OMAR!

"GO! GO!" he turned to yell to me as he waved his hand for me to leave. His body shook as the slugs decorated his chest. He fell back and out the window from the force of being shot.

"Omar! Oh my God!

The bullets continued to fly as the side and back windows were shoot out. I leaned on the gas pedal and made my escape. I immediately called his family and they rushed over. The police were on sight by the time they got there. Omar was decapitated and a victim of a war between the African syndicate and the Philly Cartel. I was scared to death and I immediately went into hiding. It was total of One hundred thousand dollars in hidden in the boiler and I gave them back the suitcase full of heroin. With Omar now gone I really needed to do for myself. In the time that I was with him he showed me so much. I was not a little girl anymore. I was at crossroad in my life and decided that I would open my own business.

HEADGAME   by Brandy
You win some you lose some

Six months after Omar's passing and I still couldn't get him out of my system. He did as he promised and made sure that I was well taken care of. He left me a hundred thousand cash and a deed to a building in North Philly. His father Jamal was out for blood and vengeance for those that assassinated his young son. The Africans killed Omar because he shot the leaders son while attempting to collect a debt for his father. The young African was shot in the leg and put out a contract on Omar and before they knew it war was being declared. The bodies where piling up in alleyways throughout the city. The blood bath lasted for six months and I stayed around Omar's family despite the warring. His mother Khadija and Jamal treated as if I was family. They had taken me in as if I was the daughter they never had. I was invited to all the Philly Cartel functions and sat with the head family.

Khadija took her son's lost very difficult as she collapsed in the street. She was hurried to the hospital as the shock weighed heavy on her. That night I sat with her as we cried together and hugged. We were both in a bad emotional condition. I was still in shock about almost being killed. The feelings of guilt where eating me alive because I felt like he gave is life to save me. Omar and I were close and planned on building a life together. We talked about settling down with kids but that was just a dream now.

HEADGAME   *by Brandy*

Omar dreamed of opening up a legitimate business and talked about owning some shops. He loved his family and adored his mother. He wanted to impress his father and prove that he was just as tough. Jamal attempted to lead Omar out of the family business but he refused. He never got the opportunity to do what he wanted so I decided that I would make his dream mine. I hired carpenters and contractors to completely renovate the store fronts. It took them six months to open the business and to acquire all the licenses. I had the protection of Jamal and Philly Cartel to operate our business. I opened a hair salon, barbershop with a speakeasy in the back. This became a frequent after hour spots for Philly Cartel captains and Lieutenants to hangout. A full bar sat in the corner next to the stripper's pole so the dancers could do their thang. The tables where scattered about as the DJ spinned on the turn tables playing the latest sound he had to offer. It wasn't a large place but I was able to run a profitable business. A lot of the Philly Cartel's supporter arrived nightly drinking and gambling. I met a lot of people that came by the shops and received many invitations to go out on dates but I never accepted.

Jamal and the Africans finally decided to have a ceasefire after six months of warring. The body counts had risen to 25 people dead and 15 wounded. The Feds decided to investigate the homicides and begun poking around in the family business. The investigation caused the two crews a lot of attention and the loss of millions of dollars. The Africans leader son was killed in a drive by

HEADGAME *by Brandy*

shooting. The two sects decided to call it quits because they lost enough, blood and money.

It was too difficult to date after Omar's death. I had been adopted by Omar's family and spent my free time with them. I didn't focus on meeting anybody because it was easier being me. Anyhow once a guy found out that I was part of the Philly Cartel they immediately ran off especially when I mentioned Jamal. They were afraid and scared to offend his Dad. I didn't want to look for someone else because Omar shoes were hard to fill. He must have felt my apprehension and told me that I was still young and I need to live my life. He tried to encourage moving on but I stayed alone.

My reputation as bein a bitch and acting like a spoiled Diva preceded me. Rumors started around the bar that I thought I was to good for them. People would secretly accuse me of being conceded for not allowing myself to open up to them. I wanted to meet some one with the same status as Omar or as influential. My decision to keep to myself and not fuck wit anybody made me very lonely.

Friday and Saturdays nights at the speakeasy was where all the real high rollers would show up. This is when I got to see what niggas was really workin with. What cars they driven? What they liked to drink? What jewelry they sported? I'd sit on the side and watch them walk around the room spendin money and talkin big shit.

HEADGAME   by Brandy

I wasn't sure if I wanted to date a baller because I didn't want to go through losing someone again. Everybody I came to love left me and I was beginning to feel unlucky. I seem to only care about the money and what a guy could do for me. Now that my financial status changed I was considered looking for some square to date. I pictured dating a doctor, lawyer or somebody with a regular nine to five. Who am I trying to kid? I was addicted to life and loved every second of it. I was gonna have to go for a bigger fish.

I had fifty thousand in cash saved and was netting five thousand a week from the businesses. The hair shops were bringing in 2000 a week, while the speakeasy brought in the rest. We only served the best liquor and food for all occasions. A team of strippers would show up on the weekends and give private dances to the patrons. The music would thump and the cash was tossed up on the stage. I admired the dancers as they bravely shook their asses and gathered the money together.

It was my 19th birthday and my girls decided that they were going to throw me a fancy all out party. The hottest DJ was hired to spend the one's and two's. I had an ice sculpture of some bird made and cases of Patron, Cirock and Hennessy. I ordered the waiters to let no glass be empty. I spent eight hours getting my hair braided in micros and my scalp was sore as shit. The caterer fixed some bangin ass food: chicken, fish, ribs, baked Mac & cheese and collared greens. I put on my

HEADGAME   *by Brandy*

sexiest Yves Saint Laurent dress with the back out and with come fuck me pumps. I was waxed, dipped and some more shit. It was VIP only and all the high rollers from the Philly Cartel showed up with gifts and for the first time in a while I felt like I was special. I loved that feeling and wished I could always have be like this.

"Oh that's my shit," as I ran to the dance floor waving my glass.

"I want to luv you PYT, Pretty young thing, you needs some luvin TLC," The speaker's rang out.

I proceeded to shake my ass and throw it hard to the loud music. I was being watched by the men in the crowd but I didn't care. When I arrived at my table there where three bottles of champagne waiting for me

"Oh my god girl, look all this stuff," Margi replied. Margi was my home girl that I knew since high school. She hung out with me and consoled me ever since the passing of Omar. Margi is one of the most sought after hair stylist in Philly. She was the heart and soul of my shop. It was her connections and her talent that filled the hair shop daily. I really didn't know anything about the hair business. We'd become close and gained a real trust for one another. I loved her style and taste in clothing, hair and jewelry. She became my personal stylist and was responsible for my Diva ness look. All my stylish dresses, outfits and heels I wore were her idea. She even dressed me for my party. I was wearing a small black dress with

HEADGAME   by Brandy

spaghetti straps that was giving a whole a lot of cleavage and damn it's having the right effect. I couldn't move with out being followed around by some hanger on.

I decided to make my rounds at the party and thank my guest for coming. I was introduced as the daughter of Jamal and Khadija Abdula, leaders of the Philly Cartel. Some people were at the party that I never seen before where handing me all types of gifts. Margi walked beside me as our hands where filled with cards containing money. The most impressive gift was from a king pin named Donnie "Da Black Scarface" Williams. His three carat diamond pedant sparkled as the light reflected it. While staring at it my pussy became dripping wet. I was like damn and my eyebrows rose when I saw it. I didn't want him to see me drooling over those gorgeous stones but I couldn't help it.

It was rumored that he was worth millions of dollars and supplied dope from Connecticut to Florida. He was a close member of the family whom I had seen around. His reputation was almost godly and he was available. Jamal and Donnie did a lot of business together. Donnie was supplying Jamal with Heroin since the connection with Africans dried up. During the warring I could remember them talking on the phone a lot. Donnie supplied Jamal with guns and intelligence.

This was my first time looking at him and he wasn't sore on the eyes. Donnie was no sucker and just the right kind of king pin I needed to get with. I

HEADGAME by Brandy

wasn't gonna throw myself at him but he was rich and I needed that in my life. I wanted to get my chance with him and needed to figure out how I was gonna do it. I knew bitches where chasin him. So I had to step up my game.

I ran back to the dance floor as the DJ pumped out the music. I danced till my feet hurt and I was barefoot. The party was still goin till 4 am and the strippers where still shakin their shit left and right. I was tired as shit and really wanted to end the party but these mutha fucka's where gettin it in. Margi must have recognized my defeat and whispered in my ear.

"Go ahead girl I'll make sure everything is closed up" Margi remarked I clinched my bag eased out the back door to make my escape. I searched my bag for my car key and I soon remember I left them in my office. I dreaded the idea of goin back in because I would have to escape all over again.

"Shit," I slammed my butt against the door and folding my arms in frustration

"Excuse me," a deep voice called out. I ain't pay that shit any mind and ignored him all altogether.

"Excuse me Miss are you aight," again the voice called out. I was ready to say some slick shit out my mouth when I noticed the caller was no other than Donnie. I switched gears fast and put my best smile on.

HEADGAME   by Brandy

"Oh, I didn't know it was you. Are you followin me?" looking him straight up and down. I resisted grabbing this fine ass nigga and doin him right here. But instead I played the damsel in distress mode.

" I can't find my car keys," as I twisted my mouth sideways.

"Damn girl you don't need to make your face like that. Maybe I can give u a ride home?" he rubbed his chin.

"OK!" I yelled excitedly.

"Aight then let's go," He added as we walked toward his car. I immediately focused in on his large feet and plump ass. I wanted to squeeze his buns tightly. Donnie was six foot two inches with a muscular physic, a dark complexion and a swagger that radiated. I was hypnotized while walking to his car. A black *Aston Martin was a waiting our* arrival. I only saw those in a James Bond movie and a Puffy video.

I sunk into the butter leather seats and crossed my legs cuz a bitch was turned the fuck on. He wore crusted diamonds, eel skin shoes and the smell of polo cologne ignited my sense. I gave him my simple directions to my address.

"I hope your father Jamal don't be trippin when he hears about me takin you home," as he grinned showing his polished teeth.

HEADGAME *by Brandy*

"he ain't gonna mind that, beside ain't ya'll aight" I quickly corrected him.

"We cool but I hope he dont feel no way about that".

"What about your wife aint she gonna worry about you bein out this late,"

"I'm not married and if I was you wouldn't be in this car I'm a one woman and I just ain't found the right lady yet,"

We talked about the Philly Cartel and the war being over. He talked of his relationship with Jamal and how he was going to be staying in Philadelphia for awhile. It was good news to hear and I hoped we get a chance to see much more of each other. He parked in front my house and I slowly opened the door to get out.

"Maybe you and I could go out some time"

"That sounds nice what did you have it in mind"

"I gotta make sure it's alright with Jamal, you understand"

"I do understand"

"but meanwhile take my number so we can stay in touch" can I use your phone," He asked as he looked around. I handed him my phone and he dial his number. He wished me a good night without even tryin anything. I knew from there that he was

HEADGAME *by Brandy*

going to be mine. I could tell by the way he looked at me that he wanted to sex me. Before we could take it further we would have to make sure it was alright with the family. I still depended on Jamal's support and to not give him the proper respect could result into problems. I anticipated when Donnie would talk with Jamal about seeing me. I could only hope it would be soon. I was excited at my new prospects and how it would turn out for me. I stood half the night thinkin of how a great couple we would make. I finally was ready to dooze off to sleep and then I mumbled these famous words.

"You win some and you lose some"

HEADGAME   *by Brandy*

Are You Still Down For ME

RING! RING! RING! RING! The phone sounded over and over. I tried to ignore it by pulling the cover over my eyes but it kept on blaring aloud. My head was pounding as my hangover took precedence. It felt as if the phone was sitting on top of my head and sounding off inside my ears. The loud ringing continued until I couldn't ignore it any longer. I turned over and snatched the phone off the receiver. I was angry at whoever was calling me so feverishly.

HEADGAME by Brandy
"Yes!"

"Oh bitch I was ready call the cops. When I saw your car was parked outside the bar I thought somebody kidnapped or killed ya," Margi said.

"No, I got a ride home from Donnie,"

"Yah nasty bitch! Did ya fuck him? Did ya put ur thang on him too ?"

"It was just a ride that's all it ways, I'm okay just got a little hangover," I responded.

"Is he there with you? Now don't be a stingy gimme the details, I need details." She quickly fired question after question hoping to get a response out of me.

"ain't nothing happen and keep who drove me home to yourself"

"Nothing happened"

I can tell that Margi was surprised that I didn't do anything with Donnie. It was complicated and I had to wait before I made my move on him. It was a momentary defeat but I had a feeling that I would be getting my second chance.

"oh you must be losing your touch," She squealed out as she sprinkled salt on the wound. I sucked it in and dare not reply. I did not want to reveal that he was going to Jamal for permission. I was angry because she was trying to clown me. It wasn't

HEADGAME by *Brandy*

everyday that I got passed over like yesterdays bread. She'd pushed a button because I was used to getting what I wanted. I liked being in control and I didn't take rejection well. I feared that Jamal would refuse his request and I would have to turn Donnie away. The more I thought about him the more I wanted him more. Margi continued questioning me but I avoided giving up the details.

Every Sunday the Abdullah family would have dinner together. I hadn't missed a dinner since I've known them. Khadija was a great cook and loved to make large meals for her extensive family. Her Son, their wives, and only the closet of friend were invited. The guys watched the football game as the girls piled into the kitchen cooking and talking. I would spend quality time with them it was like having family of my own. I didn't like spending Sundays by myself besides if I didn't show up I would never hear the end of it.

I showered and dressed for the family gathering. I was the first to arrive at the house. Khadija was sitting in the kitchen brewing over a pot of collard greens and smoke neck bones. While Jamal slumped is his large lazy boy chair dozing in and out of sleep. The large flat screen tv rumbled from the surround sound as the commercials viewed. When Khadija came to the door I hugged her tightly and gave her a warm greeting.

"Hey Mom howya doin"

"Hello Vickey! How was your party?

HEADGAME by Brandy

"It was fine, just fine, I wished you'd and Poppa could have made it"

"We to old to be out there clubbin witya young folks"

"I still wished y'all was there"

"I know sweetie but Poppa gotya a little somethin and don't tell em I told you

"Okay, I won't tell...Mmm what's cookin in the kitchen"

I could smell the baked barbecue chicken in the oven as I walked into the kitchen. Momma asked me to shred the cheese while sitting with her. We worked on the food as the family slowly arrived Jamal Jr, his two kids and his wife showed. The house was buzzing with life as the Philadelphia Eagles played football.

While the table was being prepared a special guest had arrived without my knowledge. Donnie was sitting in the living room beside Jamal talking. I was truly surprised at his attendance and didn't expect to see him so soon. I gasped as he smiled at me and flirted from a distance. I was blushing as he caught me eyes looking at him. The girls talked about him as if he was a rock star. Momma could tell there was something brewing by the look in my eye. It was long time since they seen me so giddy and lively. However, before dinner was served we where able to talk briefly.

HEADGAME *by Brandy*

"Ah Vickey it's nice to see you again"

"Oh is it"

"Do you still want me to talk to Jamal about us?"

"If you want me to"

"Yes I do and I'll be takin care of that, after dinner"

The large wooden table was filled with people as they scarfed down the food. Jamal sat at the head of the table and observed his family. He was proud man and took pride in everything he did. The conversation was kept to a minimum as the food swiftly disappeared. The light where dimed and they startled me with theri singing.

"Happy Birthday to you"

"Happy Birthday to you

"Happy Birthday dear Vickey"

"Happy Birthday to you"

I cried as Momma arrived holding a large cake. Poppa held me next to him and gave me a small box. The cake was cut as I ripped open the gift. It was a diamond ring that fit my finger perfectly.

"Thank you, Thank you Poppa"

I reached and gave Jamal the tightest hug possible. I was grateful to him for supporting me. It was an emotional moment for me as I was

HEADGAME   by Brandy

overcome with gratitude. Since they took me in and treated me as there own. I sobbed loudly because it had been such a long time since someone cared about me. By the time I finished crying and creating a scene everybody around joined in. We ate the cake while Jamal and Donnie was sitting on the porch. No one could hear what they was talkin about but I was assuming it was about my future. I tried to read Poppa's lips but I was unable to see them. Momma caught wind of what I was doin and pulled me aside.

"Let them handle their business come help me with the dish's"

I did as I was told and helped momma in the kitchen. I started to wash dishes with her and anxiuosly waited for Donnie. He opened the screen door and came toward me.

"He said if it's okay with you we can go out on a date"

"OKAY!" "OKAY!"

I was truly happy and couldn't wait for our date. The day ended well and I made my way home. I sat on the bed and stared at the walls wondering when Donnie would come see me. I drifted into a light sleep and was awaken by a familiar sound.

I heard my ring tone playing and that prompted me to look for my bag. I quickly pulled it out and flipped it open. The caller ID displayed a number I never seen before but I reluctantly press talk.

HEADGAME   by Brandy

"Hello?" waiting for a reply.

"Ms Diamond, could you please hold a minute Mr. Williams would to have a word with you," The professional sounding lady replied.

"Who is that?"

"Mr. Donnie Williams would like to talk to you please hold,"

I didn't want be rude so I waited and when the phone beeped he answered the phone.

"Vickey, howya doin are you ready for our date", He asked.

"Yes! I hope we can do something nice," I asked sounding a little over anxious.

"Well I hoped that we could go get something to eat in Center City wouldya like that"

"That's sounds so nice"

"Be ready tomorrow at 8pm and dress to impress" He answered in a confident voice.

"I'll be ready, bye"

"Later"

I was so excited that I rolled over the bed screaming. I needed to share this information with Margi. When she answered the phone I rubbed my date in her face. Margi was excited and wished

HEADGAME   *by Brandy*

me well but I could tell she was jealous by the tone of her voice. I got cold feet for a minute because it seemed like ages since I been out with someone. She reminded of the gift certificate for the spa I received for my birthday. It was for a full day of pampering at the spa. Once I finished there I'd feel like new women.

The next morning I hurried to the Spa so I could begin my scheduled pampering and cleansing. It was beautiful inside the spa and had everything I needed inside. The marble floors shined and the giant glass mirrors reflected my image. It showed how much I was in need of their services. I changed into a terry cloth bathrobe and shower slippers. I entered a private room where I'd receive a special mud bath with organic mud.

After the mud bath, facial, full manicure and pedicure I headed to the hair shop to get a touch up on my braids. I anticipated the outfit Margi selected for me. Margi had very good sense of fashion and always knew how to hook up an outfit.

Even though I knew she was a envious of my looks, she was no competition. Her skin had very bad acne but she was pretty hair. Her ass was fatter then mine but so was her stomach too. She was cool as shit and had great taste in clothing. Her color coordination was exceptional and she knew how to dress a bitch right. When I arrived at the shop it was buzzing with gossip and all thanks to Margi. She informed them that I was dating the much sought after Donnie. These bitches ain't never pay me no kind of mind but all of a sudden I

HEADGAME   by Brandy

was an instant rock star. The girls waved and hi five me like it was a wedding.

"Damn you bitches need to mine ur own business "Margi stated as she dragged me off to the back. She handed me the sexiest dress I saw. It was a one of kind Vera Wang knee high length black sequence dress with spaghetti straps and pair of black patent leather pumps with the toes out. I added the diamond chocker, his pedant and my new diamond ring to match. I dressed at the salon because Margi wouldn't have it no other way. She poked, pulled and sprayed till every piece of cloth and hair was in order. When I approached the mirror I hardly recognized the Diva that stood before me. I was hot and I hoped Donnie thought so to.

I quickly dashed home and awaited his arrival. My cell phone rang and it was Donnie telling me to come outside. I arrived outside to find him waiting for me in a cherry red Ferrari. I slowly walked toward the car giving him every opportunity to see what I was wearing. He raised the door and I melted inside the car. He was dressed in some top of the line Rocawear linen suit.

"So where are we goin?" I asked.

"Maggio's , I hope you like Italian"

"I love it!"

HEADGAME   by Brandy
"Well let's go"

  We drove through Fairmount Park and quickly arrived on the expressway. He raved the engine loudly and shifted the gears. The Ferrari jump into gear and took off like a lion running for its prey. RRRRRRMMM! The car jerk forward as I watched the speedometer moving swiftly past the number 75 Mph mark. He shifted the car into gear again it was moving past 95 MPH mark. My heart was already beating fast and palms where sweaty as he skillfully raced in and out of traffic. We pasted the slower cars at a rate so high that they were a blur. The car continued to excel as the speedometer reached 180 mph. I held on to the side door and closed my eyes praying. I wanted to scream stop but instead I edged him on.

"Oh baby is that all this thing can do"

"Oh so you like speed"

"Yes I do. Can you make it hit 200"

"Shit Imma try"

He pulled the gear back again and the car jump forward to 200 mph. I was excited at the feat and I never drove this fast before. A loud buzzing sounded a warning that police radar was a attempting to track the car. He quickly slowed the car to the legal speed limit. After a couple of traffic lights we were parking in front Maggio's.

HEADGAME   by Brandy

When we arrived at Maggio's we sat in the small booth in the rear. It was a dimly lit and very romantic. It reminded me of the restaurants in the throwback mafia movies.

"So tell me about you," He asked.

"Im just getting over a tragic relationship with Jamal's son Omar. I was their when he got killed. My Dad was killed last year and my mother was shipped to the crazy house. She didn't handle his passing well. I'm alone and all I got is me"

"Well that rough but know you got me and I'm gonna make it all better"

"Is that right?

"Yes it is"

"why do they call him da black scarface?"

"I shot a whole block up with two ak-47s. I waved them around shouting Say hello to little friend," he answered gesturing like he was holding the guns.

"NO WAY!"

"No, I'm jokin," He replied smirking while noticing my shock.

"Come on,"

"OK, when I was kid I just used watch Scarface movie all time and act like I Tony Montana. So

HEADGAME *by Brandy*

when I got in the game the name stuck, Now if tell anybody that story I'm gonna deny it." He replied stuffing large amount of food in his mouth. After we finished our meal we set out for an upscale nightclub. The manager shuffled us through crowd to the VIP area. A very famous rapper was given a private album release partly. He shouted Donnie out and waved his mike in the air.

"Yo dis fo mi homey Da Black Scarface," the rapper spit out and begun to sing his entire song over. Donnie didn't let me out of his sight and I made sure that I didn't wonder far from him. I took pictures with the famous rapper and his crew. I was treated like a celebrity and it was all because I was with him. I felt like if I was snow white. I was straight trippin from the door. The night went into the later part of the evening he introduced me as his lady and I didn't stop him

By the time he drove me home I was ready for some of his dick but was he willing to give it to me. I didn't care if it was too soon and all that other shit but i just had to go for mine. We not only fucked but our mind, body and soul was joined together. I wanted to feel his rock hard dick beating out my pussy. I especially loved the way his balls slapped the back of my ass. He twisted my legs over my head, folded them sideways and banged it from the back. It was a Burger King night "have it his way," I aint gonna lie I rode him like a cowgirl and when I finished I swallowed his load. I watched his toes bend and his back arch. By the time I was finished wit him he was sleep. I rolled over and heard the

HEADGAME   *by Brandy*

radio playing Jon B and Tupac record," *Are You Still Down For ME"*. For that moment on we were down for each other.

The Gift and the Curse

We took our time to get to know each other. We were together every night. It was like deja vu and I was falling in love all over again. I loved they way he treated me and how took care of me. When he was around I had nothing to neither fear nor worry about. We clicked as we laughed, danced and shared quality time together. I was riding a cloud and dare not jump off it

Jamal and Khadija would ask me how we where doing and I had nothing but good things to report. I was so happy that I was given a second chance to love. I had no remorse about how things turned out but I wished it was different circumstances between Donnie and I. With Omar gone I had to

HEADGAME   *by Brandy*

change my life and grow up faster than expected. My life was good and my suffering seemed to never exist. There was confidence in my step and a glow in my eyes like never before. I was feeling brand new and it was all thanks to Donnie.

Things between Donnie and I heated up so fast that we were unofficially living together. I was ready to give up my place without question. I didn't care about the security I had from having my own spot. His well being become most important I was in love and I needed to be his like he was mine. I no longer desired my life of solitude I was ready for a partnership. Being with Donnie made me no longer plan for the worst because through his eyes I had the best.

It was during the Sunday dinner at Jamal's and Khadijah that he presented me with a most serious proposal. I know that he was feeling me like I was feeling him. We ate our usual Sunday meal with all the trimmings that Khadija prepared. I shoveled a pile of macaroni in my mouth as the he stood banging his glass with his fork.

"Cling, cling, cling" the tapping of the glass sounded.

"Can I have everyone's attention....I want to first thank you for accepting me as part as the family, second I want to say this to Vickey..I love you babe and since I've known you I've been the most happiest in my life. I ...I.... I... wanna know If you'll marry me?"

HEADGAME   *by Brandy*

He opened a box containing a large diamond engagement ring and flashed it across the table. I gasped for air and couldn't believe what he asked of me. I sat silently with my mouth open; it took a push for Momma to snap me back into the reality. He was awaiting my answer.

"Yes! Yes! I accept!

I jump up and made my way over to him at break neck speed. We embraced as I gave him the sloppiest kiss possible. He placed the ring on my finger to signal our engagement has begun. Poppa Jamal nodded his head in agreement as he watched us holding each other. I wondered if he had something to do with but it really didn't matter. I was so happy that tears of Joy strayed down my cheeks. I modeled my ring for the girls as they envied the size of the rock. After his proposal I did what any loyal fiancé did I moved in. With engagement and our wedding to take place in the summer nothing could make me happier. I was now exalted to Wifey status ridding high and never wanting to come down.

He had several apartments and properties all over town. Our main place is in a high rise down in Center City but I would frequently stay at a stash house out in Upper Darby. It was small quiet house that attracted little attention. It was the house that I pictured in my dreams. While traveling around the city he was so careful to the point that it made my sick. His constant changing of plans took a toll on my nerves. He doubled back, drove scenic routes to ensure we weren't being followed. He'd search

HEADGAME   *by Brandy*

his car for microphone and hidden camera's. Sometimes we'd pull in front of our destination and speed right off because he had some kind of bad vibes. He always tells me that he only trusted me and his vibes. If he didn't get a good vibe somewhere he would roll out. The life was unforgiving so we needed to be vigilant at all times.

His main crew consisted of four men that carried money and dope to specific spots. It was the twins Hassan and Rasaan, Andrew and Chyna. I never got to meet the twins. They are two young boys out of North Philly. He kept them far away from the house because they were careless and to flashy, that's what Donnie always talks about. Donnie didn't trust them because they were young, ambitious and cold blooded. He loved their work but knew to keep them on a long leash. They could turn around and bite you at any given time.

He kept the twins away from us and I only met Chyna and Andrew on special occasions. He slowly brought his people around so I could see them. However, I still didn't have chance to talk to anyone. It was six months into our engagement that he finally introduced me to Andrew his 1st in command and confident. Andrew was alright lookin dude that dropped off money. At first he didn't say much but as time went on he opened up. He was totally loyal to Donnie and did anything he told him to do. They where childhood friends and seemed inseparable. I could tell that there relationship was deeper than it appeared. I couldn't put my finger on exactly what it is but time will tell. Sometimes Donnie would scream at Andrew like that was his

HEADGAME   *by Brandy*

kid and I assumed Andrew was gonna scream back at him but he swallowed his tongue. I disliked Andrew for not standing up for himself. I never got in between their disagreement even though I paid close attention. Andrew spent a lot of time at the casinos gambling his earning and when he was broke he asked Donnie for loans. Money was always at the root of their arguments.

Occasionally Andrew and his girl Chyna would come over to socialize. When they came over for dinner and drinks we played spades. Chyna and I were the reigning champs as we bust their ass. So far we won 10 games to their two wins. The rule was no business talk but somehow it seemed to get slipped in. I would immediate interrupt them before it got too deep. They would drink Henny and smoke blunts until the room was filled with smoke. I didn't smoke weed but I loved the way it smelled. I seen how people reacted after they smoked weed and they acted goofy. The weed they smoke was hydroponically grown and 3 times more potent then any weed that was around. This hydroponically grown weed smelled of grapes, strawberry and cherry. I was attempted to try it but I was quickly reminded of my family's addiction and its consequences.

The guns, bullet proof vest and secret life was hard at first but I got used to it. Our condo was filled with cash that was stacked in the bedroom. I learned that money has a stinky smell and no amount of incense could cover the it. I wore gloves when I touched money because I noticed my hands would be filthy after handling it for a couple

HEADGAME   *by Brandy*

of hours. The sound of money counting machine zipped all through the night as the large sums of cash where counted and stack. Donnie and Andrew loaded suitcases and garbage cans with cash. I got sick of seeing and smelling it. The dope business seemed to never stopped as piles of money grow bigger and bigger.

Not only did he have to hide drugs, he had to move around money from stash house to stash house. I like the stash house out in Upper Darby because he only put money and small arms there. Nobody in his crew knew about this house. Donnie kept his where about secret and if he didn't answer his phone I wouldn't know if he was alive. Sometimes he disappeared for a couple hours at a time. When I'd asked him what he was doing he reply's that he was taking care of business. Maybe I was being over sensitive but sometimes I got a feeling that something else was going on. I hoped that he wasn't cheating me or seeing somebody else behind my back. I confided in Chyna about my feelings of insecurity and ask for her advice. She reassured me that anything was going on and I should trust his words.

I couldn't get enough of this nigga, he put it on me so good I was dick whipped. I was giddy and child like when I was with him. If he'd ask me I would have gone through hell and high water for him. He put me so high up on a pedestal that I never wanted to come down. The material things where nice but the power and position was intoxicating.

HEADGAME   *by Brandy*

When I drove through the hood bitches greeted me as if I was a star. While at the hair salon those same bitches that turned up their noses now smiled and kissed my ass. I become drunk with the power and addicted to the control. If I was to even raise my voice to a nigga fear was transparent on their face. Nigga's dare not cross me or try me because of whom I represented. When I stepped into the room I commanded respect. I was determined to keep my position and bury anyone who tried to take it away. The entire hood treated my like I was that Diva and I played my part well. I strutted around in large hats and Dolce & Gabana shades like I was Beyonce. I even paid for blond shoulder length extensions in my hair. I would roll my neck letting the curls slap me all over my face. I was able to have anything and do anything that I wanted. The Car dealer let me drive off the lot with a different car weekly. I was changin Cars so rapidly that people couldn't keep up with what I was driving. I loved when we went on shopping trips to New York and splurging on jewelry, clothes and shoes. Tiffany's was my favorite jewlry store, I spent hours there. I would meet up with my cousin Jessie and she'd accompany on my trips when Donnie was out on business.

Africans and the Philly Cartel started warring again. Donnie was worried that somebody may try to kidnap me due to my associations with them. Some Africans were spotted in the parking lot of my speakeasy. They tried to kidnap a member of the Philly Cartel. Jamal ordered we have armed protection.

HEADGAME *by Brandy*

Donnie responded by having Andrew to escort me every place I'd go. Andrew was a tall slender brotha with tight curls and very good looking. However his soft demeanor made him unattractive to me. I didn't like how Donnie treated him so disrespectful it was like he wasn't able to stick up for himself. Donnie demanded anywhere I go I had to be escorted. I didn't like the idea of Andrew following me around but we both didn't have a choice. Andrew would be in so much trouble if anything ever happened to me on his watch. Andrew was engaged to Chyna a Puerto Rican beauty. She had long black hair, hazel eyes and a body that mirrored Buffy. I could see why Andrew was attracted her; she is all bit of beautiful. She spoke like a common New Yorkrican with a strong spanglish accent. Her unibrow was arched nicely and her hair was down to her back with long black waves. She spent a lot of time at the shop catching us up with the latest hood gossip. I didn't mind her company and thought she lightened up the crowd up. I didn't mind her loud, foot stomping ghetto antics. However Margi and Chyna were not so fond of each other and constantly talked about each other behind their backs. It was stressful maintaining their friendships but somehow I did. Margi didn't take well to Chyna.

"I don't trust that heifer and you shouldn't either" Margi warned me and waved her finger. I ignored her and told her she was being paranoid. After all Chyna hadn't done anything to me that caused me to worry about her. She was a little obnoxious at times but I liked her.

HEADGAME   by Brandy

Donnie and I decided we needed a vacation, so we invited Andrew and Chyna for a seven day Cruise on the Majestic, a four star cruise to Jamaica Montego bay. When drank, gambled and partied all the way to Jamaica. Donnie paid for us to go sightseeing while Andrew and Chyna went off shopping. I didn't understand how they were doin anything because Andrew had the fever for the dice and already lost over twenty thousand cash. He was into Donnie for half of that.

When it came time to meet the tour Donnie felt sick and decided not to go. I so baldly wanted to shop for gold bangles and eat some real smoked jerk chicken. We stop at a couple of shops and I spent some cash there. An hour into the tour an unsuspecting storm came. The tour continued move on but not with me. I don't do the rain thing and I already brought my bangles. Having the jerk chicken wasn't that serious so I quickly made it back to the ship. Our suite was on the top of the ship with two rooms and a balcony. My outfit was soaked and my nipples were sticking out. I slid the pass key throw the lock and the green light signaled that it was open. I pushed the door and went straight for the bathroom. I reached for the towel so I could dry off.

"*Ooooooh Ohhhhhh Shit, baby,*' I heard coming from the bedroom. I lifted my ear toward the moaning. I walked slowly to the door and my eyes focused in on Chyna and Donnie fucking. She was lying on her back with her legs folded behind her

HEADGAME — by Brandy

head. He was sweating profusely and grunting like a wild animal. My life flashed before my eyes and I didn't let out a word. I covered my mouth and slowly backed out of the door. I ran to the bar begging the bartender for a drink.

"Gimme a triple shot of Henny,"

I contemplated my next move and thought about how I was gonna get over this.

"Fuck!"

I thought about the situation and I came to the conclusion that I didn't want to ruin a good vacation. I would act as if I didn't see anything. I was sore at him and I pretended it never happened: at least until I reached the United States soil.

A woman's scorn

When we arrived in the states I was so angry at him that I didn't know what to do. My feelings and ego was hurt as I thought of his betrayal constantly. I tried to act like it never existed but I knew the truth and the truth will set me free. I was lucky to have some one to confide in but that didn't ease my pain.

It was my girl Margi that helped me bare this burden. I was sadden even more as I told her about seeing Donnie and Chyna fuckin. The tears covered my face as I cried out in frustration. The arrogance was gone from my swagger as I pictured them sweating and humping. I wondered if the people around me knew of his infidelities and was laughing behind my back. I was no longer feeling like Vickey the King Pins wifey but a joke to laugh at. I entrusted Jessie with my humiliation and her face hit the floor. She didn't believe me but the tears of seriousness on my face allowed her to accept my painful reality. She grabbed her straight razor and threatened to cut this bitch's face. She encouraged me to call the bitch over to the shop

HEADGAME *by Brandy*

and we beat that bitch's ass. Momentarily I agreed with her but this attack would create a lot of shit and it would hell to pay from Donnie. I stopped myself from trying to hurt her at least physically but I was gonna get even some other way. Margi picked up the phone and begun to dial Chyna's number but I stopped her after she pressed the first four digits. I let her know that I was gonna get even with her ass in a very special way because I had some other shit on my mind. I was sore about all the laughin and giggling this bitch was doing in my face. I wasn't just upset that he was givin away my dick but how devious and deceitful they were about it. I decided that I was gonna give a nigga taste of his own medicine. My revenge will be brutal and painful to those who chose to betray my trust. It took time to convince Margi not to say anything. I threaten her and swore Margi to silence. I promised her that if she leaked a word out not only would I fire her ass but I would put a contract out on her life. I hated to be like that but that was the only way I could get this bitch to button her lips. She tried to smirk like it was a joke but I assured her that I was more serious than a heart attack. Understanding that it was a matter best kept to herself she promised that she would kept it a secret.

As we talked amongst ourselves Chyna parked her car in front of the salon. Margi and I gazed at each other as we watched her closely. I gave Margi a serious look to signal that I was not playing and to follow my lead. I caught a glimpse of myself in the mirror and the fire in my eyes. I looked as my mother once did. My anger brought out the dark

HEADGAME   *by Brandy*

qualities that I tried so hard to cover up. Chyna pushed the door open and greeted us with a joyous smile. She acted as if all was cool and I kept it going that way.

"Hey girl howya doin?"

"I'm good, what's new witya"

"I was wondering if you could give a wash and set?"

"I'm busy but Margi can take care of ya"

"Ooh, I like the way you do it"

"Don't worry she gotya"

"Aight then"

Chyna sat in the chair and allowed Margi to fix her hair. Margi didn't say much of anything but I wanted to strangle her on the spot. While washing her hair, Margi picked a bottle of lye and started to put it in her hair. This would cause her scalp to get chemically burned and her hair to fall out by the clumps. I moved my finger across my throat signaling death if she went on with her plan. Margi showed some self control by completing the job without incidence. I was proud of her and I promised that I will show her my appreciation on a later date.

My patience and tolerance were wearing thin and I was so upset that I cringed in agony when Donnie

HEADGAME   by Brandy

touched me. I made all kinds of excuses not to fuck him and he was growing very impatient. I'd claim my stomach was hurting and I was having my period. I used the period excuse so much that I should have bled to death by now. I was on strike and it was no pussy for him. We'd stay up talking while in bed and I'd ask him questions about our relationship.

"Would you ever cheat on me," I asked sincerely.

"I'd never do such a thing to you, I love you Vee!"

"Do you want somebody else?

"I don't want anybody but you Vee,"

I almost hoped that he came clean with me but like a true punk ass nigga he denied it and swore up and down that he'd never hurt me. He swore his eternal love for me but I was unconvinced by his lying and twisting the truth. Then just to fuck with him I'd make remarks about Chyna. I'd watch for a reaction and gestures to my accusations. No matter what I said he didn't react. I was driving myself mad as his lies continue to hurt me deeper. I wanted him to feel the agony, embarrassment and the pain he was putting me through.

Mother Khadija called me at the shop and requested that I have lunch with her. We met at a small restaurant in West Philly on 40th and Walnut Street. As usual Momma Khadaji was dressed elegantly in a two piece skirt set with heels and a

HEADGAME   by Brandy

mink coat. I greeted her warmly as she invited me to sit down.

"Hey Baby its nice to seeya have a seat next to mine,"

"Thanks for inviting me but this couldn't wait till Sunday"

"No baby, I needed to talk you about Donnie"

"What about Donnie?"

"Now I don't mean to get in yawls business but he's been saying ya'll havin problems, particularly female problems"

"What? I'm just not feelin well that's all"

"When you mean not feelin well do you mean in a motherly way?"

"Are askin me if I'm pregnant,"

"Well girl are you?"

"ahhh Yes... I'm six weeks now"

"I knew it! I knew it!

"Why haven't you told Donnie yet?"

"Im not ready for him to know yet and I wanna tell'em in my own little way"

HEADGAME   by Brandy

I hated to tell that lie but I needed some leverage. A pregnancy I could justify my acting differently toward him. Momma and I toasted good health and wishing me to have a baby boy. She was happy to think that she help with my problem and ready to celebrate the new family member. I knew that she would report back to Poppa Jamal that all was well. The meeting was only for an hour as we finished our meal and parted ways. I needed to buy me some time before I made my next move. I made my way back to the salon hoping I didn't make the biggest mistake of my life.

I started ciphering off cash and hiding it for rainy days. I followed the money closely and started scheming how I could take control of it. I paid more attention to Donnie's transaction and movements so I could calculate when he stored the largest sums of money in the house. I planned on using Andrew to give me more information about his business dealings.

When Andrew came to pick me up after work I sat in the front seat giving him every chance to get to know me. He never liked to talk much around me but I had my way to get him to speak. Andrew was a regular pothead and couldn't resist the smell of herbs. I would light up a rolled up blunt and pretend to smoke it. After, a few times he ignored me when I tried to pass him the blunt. He'd always shake his head no but one day I moved to pass the blunt and he instinctively grabbed it. It was the first thing we had in common and that's what I used for him to trust me. When he wasn't smokin weed he was tight lipped and didn't say much of anything.

HEADGAME   *by Brandy*

After he inhaled the cannabis I couldn't get this nigga to shut up.

"Damn, you acted like you scared to smoke wit me. Don't worry I won't tell Donnie you smoked wit me. If that's what your worried about,"

"When you started smokin, I ain't neva seen you smoke"

"Well ain't that my business or you gonna run and tell Donnie

"I don't care what you do and I'm no snitch and let me showya how to smoke this shit," He fired at me as he snatched the stick of weed out of my hand

"That's some good shit, cough! Cough! Cough!" He answered

"So tell me how long you known Donnie,"

"Oh we had been cool since we were kids. We spent time at each others home. We grew up in the same projects and I started hustlin first and I put him on. We started blowin up and I got caught delivering a gun and some coke. I did tens years for him and every since I been outta jail he's been lookin out for me. He even introduced me to my girl. THAT'S MY MAN," He blurted out.

"TEN YEARS! You did ten years for him?"

"He would have did it for me"

HEADGAME   by Brandy

He sat quietly and inhaled deeply on the potent weed. Eyes quickly turned red showing the signs of his euphoric episode kicking in.

"So this is supposed to be your empire,"

"You could say that, It was me that started all this but It ain't nothing cause we gonna take over the game as soon as we get rid of that old man Jamal"
"

"Huh"

He must of realized that what he said was dangerous because things got silent between me and him. That conversation was cut short after he tried to play it off.

"I was just jokin" he said as he toked on the blunt.

He kept smokin on that blunt and he started talking all over again. I couldn't get him to shut up. He started tellin me he disliked Donnie for bein cheap. He recalled that the new connect was his idea and how he should of gotten a bigger piece of the pie. He told me about the money stashed in the houses. I agreed with everything he said and complemented him when his idea sounded better. He'd tell me of his woman problems and what they fought about. I would always take his side of the story, so I could gain his trust. His whining was pitiful and I saw why Donnie treated him so poorly. Andrew acted like a true bitch and his attitude turned me off completely. He needed a boost of self esteem and I was willing to give to him.

HEADGAME   by Brandy

I gained Andrews confidence and avoided fights with Donnie. I put together how he was fuckin Chyyna without Andrew findin out. On the day of a full moon they would meet up and that's when Andrew was in Miami Florida taking care of business. He would lie and tell me that he was goin with him. Andrew dried snitched that info while we were talkin. I wonder how Andrew would react once he found out his girl was cheating. I decided for my plan to work I needed to recruit Andrew. I saw how he looked at me and I knew he wished for some of this sweet ass pussy. I only hoped that he be down for it.

I started a heated ass fight with Donnie over some bullshit. I tried to get him to hit me but he wasn't that type of dude. So I mistakenly hit my head on edge of the table and caused a terrible bruise. I made it look like he knocks the shit out of me. The next day when I saw Andrew I fell into his arms and cried. I rubbed my chest on him and let him feel the heat of my body. I had on the tightest skirt and when I sat in his car. It rose up to the fat of my thigh.

I held him close and told him how I survived a beaten from Donnie. He was sympathetic and held me closer to him. I made my move and leaned in for a kiss. He didn't stop me and from there we let nature take its course. It didn't take him to long to have his face in my pussy.

"OOH SHIT, EAT DAT PUSSY,"

HEADGAME   by Brandy

I squirmed like he was the best but the truth is he couldn't eat pussy to save his life. I let him do his business and when I he came up I returned the favor. I pulled his dick out his pants and to my surprise he had a nice piece. I showed him what my head games was made of. I wrapped my tongue around the head and put extra suction on it. It took only five minutes of suckin on his dick and I was taking his load. I made sure I caught it all and didn't release his dick from his mouth till I had all his cum. He shivered in ecstasy. I spit the load in a tissue, wiped my lips and fixed my hair.

After sucking his dick lovely he started beggin for my pussy. I refused to fuck him and let him know that he needed to break it off with Chyna. If he wanted some of this pussy he needed to drop that bitch like a bad habit. I demanded he do it but I was unsure that he had enough heart to go through with this matter.

I still hadn't heard anymore about the takeover of the Cartel. I listened in on Donnie calls but none of them seemed suspicious. I begun to think that what Andrew said was bullshit but Donnie met up with the twins at the house. They never came to the house and I couldn't tell what they looked like. It was late in the evening and I pretended to be sleep as they gathered in the basement to discuss their plan. I could hear every word they said as it echoed through the vents. They were going ambush Jamal while going to a meeting. I couldn't hear what day the hit would be but it was go down soon.

HEADGAME   by Brandy

Lovers and Friends

The Twins waited outside of Jamal's office from a time to strike. The all black Navigator's engine purred like a cat as it stood parked on the corner. The two man held an Ak47 with a banana clip and a chrome smith & Wesson colt 45 loaded with hollow tips aka *cop killer bullets*. The black attire from head to toe was accented with black leather gloves and ski masks to cover their faces. Hasann and Rasaan are experience stick up man and now they were adding hit squad to their resume. They weren't experienced in killing for hire but they where going to learn quickly. They figured it would be a simple task but as they soon learned that assassination is a tricky business.

It seemed like the opportunity they were waiting for would never come. The Twins were persistent and had the right motivation of $50,000 a piece. They are willing to wait until hell freezes over. Lying and

HEADGAME by Brandy

wait was very difficult job so they spent the time playing a miniature scrabble.

"B.E.A.M.A"

"That ain't any word,"

"Yeah it is, pass me the keys to my Beama"

"Get the fuck outta here! It ain't in the dictionary and it ain't a word"

"Imma check it out"

Hasan thumbed threw the dictionary and was unsuccessful at locating the word.

"See I toldya that ain't no word"

"Look there he go"

"But he's with his wife"

"It don't make me difference"

Rasaan pulled the gear into drive and the car begun to creep forward. Jamal and Khadija were walking and talking as the bodyguard followed closely behind them. Halfway down the block Hasaan slips out the car and follows behind his unsuspecting victims. The car screeched to a stop and Hassan stuck the Ak-47 out the window and released a barrage of bullets toward them. TATATATATA! The large machine gun sounded as the bullets flew out the barrel. WHISH! PING!

HEADGAME   by Brandy

SMASH! Jamal pulled Kadija to the ground sheltering his body over hers. The body guard fell to one knee and upholstered his weapon taking aim toward the car. He squeezed the trigger of his nine millimeter sending four rounds toward the car hoping to stop the sudden attack on his mentors and friends. BLOCKA, BLOCKA, BLOCKA, BLOCKA!

The bullets filled the Navigators exterior with shattered glass and metal slugs. All but one slug managed to get close to the driver as it whizzed by his ear and throw the windshield. The bodyguard emptied his weapon but to no avail he missed the mark. Rasan was standing over the body and release the large 45 slug to the head.

"BOOM! BOOM!"

Half of the body guards head flew off and his brains leaked on the concrete. He aimed the gun at Jamal as he held his hands up signaling his surrender. Jamal tried to move away from his wife but the sudden action excited the young gun man. He pointed both barrels at Jamal and squeezed the trigger without remorse. The gun smoke clouded the area and the spent shells lay over the ground. The total of sixteen shots entered Jamal's body. Five of the bullets burrowed throw him and killed Khadija. Their blood spilled onto the curve as the two gunmen made their escape.

****

HEADGAME   *by Brandy*

Chyna walked into the shop hysterically crying and hollering. I just knew the gig was up and that I was found out. If so I was gonna knock that bitch right the fuck back down.

"Its Andrew and he left me"

"What?"

"He been actin funny - like after he drops you off him is disappearing and shit...when I call his phone he don't wanna answer..."

"Nigga ain't shit, Say it ain't so"

"Imma find dat bitch and when I do Imma kick her ass"

"Poor babby, you surely don't deserve that"

"We were supposed to announce our engagement and he pull this shit"

After she said that he was going somewhere after dropping me off I wanted to laugh. I did my best not to act funny toward her and she was furious to think he was cheating on her. I wanted that bitch to hurt so badly and but I wasn't ready to rub that shit in her face. I caught myself smirking in the mirror and quickly hid it from her. Margi wanted to straight jump on her ass but I shook my head with disagreement. After all I didn't want her to know that I knew about her and Donnie. She continued to spill her guts about her love life.

HEADGAME   *by Brandy*

You bet your ass I sat in the chair and listened intently to her blabber, like I was the supportive girlfriend. She even disclosed that they where supposed to go ring shopping even though he spent all his money gambling. She promised us that she was gonna find him and they was gonna work it out again. I knew that wasn't gonna happened unless I intervened. I had Andrews head so fucked up that he'd run over his momma to get some of my good pussy. I rubbed her back all the while wishing I could stick her nasty ass with my knife. I could hardly take her dramatics any further. I left her crying and whining where she stood. I was happy to see this bitch in pain. I still wasn't satisfied so I needed to appear supportive so I decided to do what any mother fucker would and hype shit up.

"I knew that muther fucker was no good," I shouted with emotion. I appeared sympathetic and caring to my hurting friend as stage one of my payback unfolded. My attention shifted as my phone rang. It was Donnie calling and I knew that if he ever suspected dishonesty I would have to leave town on the first thing smokin.

"Hey babe"

"Hey Vee, I got something to tell you"

"What is it?"

"Jamal and Khadija was killed by the Africans"

"Oh no, Oh no, not Khadija"

HEADGAME   *by Brandy*

I cried because I wanted to warn Jamal but it was to late. I understood Donnie's eagerness to take over and I may have stood by when he killed Jamal but Khadija was an innocent bystander and didn't deserve that.

"When did it happen?"

"a half hour ago"

"Imma send Andrew to pick you up later, who's makin all that noise"

"That's Chyna over here ballin her eyes out she upset because Andrew leaving her. Do you anything about Andrew leaving her?

"I don't know nuffin , they always goin through something.

"She sayin that she goin somewhere to look for him"

"Put her ass on the phone," He commanded. I passed her the phone and he told her that she was still goin to New York to carry back cocaine for him. She needed to get her shit together and meet up with him in a hour. I tried to over hear their entire conversation but I was unsuccessful at my attempt to eavesdrop. I wasn't happy about them going to New York for an evening together. I thought it was just an excuse for them to be together. They probably were gonna stay at a hotel and fuck all night. I wanted to snatch the phone and beat the shit out of her.

HEADGAME by Brandy

I begged to go with him but he refused. I did my best sad act and pouted over the phone. I could see that she was gaining her composure and what ever Donnie told her she stopped crying. I begun thinking that she not only after my man but was trying to knock me out of my position. For the first time in the long while I was insecure and hated how it made me feel. I despised how I was bein played and made to look like a fool. I was heated but I knew if I showed my hand that I would lose it all. I resisted the temptation to call him back and cursed him. I took a deep breath, exhaled and woosa!

Chyna decided to make extra money by transporting drugs for Donnie. She'd strapped on four and five kilos of coke at time. She made numerous trips outta the country. She was capable of moving through customs and airports with ease and bravery. I tried to go with him but Donnie never put me in the middle of his business like that. He stated, *my girl don't never carry shit like that.* I concluded the only reasons she was carrying for Donnie was to impress him, she was being greedy or did for the thrill. Whatever the reason she choose she was getting in my way. As far as Donnie was concerned despite the problems she was having with her man her ass had betta be ready to carry that dope.

HEADGAME *by Brandy*

I knew their trip was more than business. Chyna had managed to get with Donnie and I was heated. It very difficult acting like I didn't care. This was the perfect opportunity to put stage two of my plan in action. I kept thinking that she was trying to knock me out the picture. For the first time in a while I was insecure and hated how it made me feel. I decided while they was gone I would put it on Andrew and get this nigga strung the fuck out on this pussy. I kept thinking of how am I going to get even with this son of a bitch.

Chyna's trip was just in time for what I needed to accomplish with Andrew. I was gonna make her pay and pay dearly she would. My mind kept obsessing and I couldn't help to think that she was gonna fuck my man all weekend. After her conversation with Donnie she left the shop to get ready for her trip. I was in pain over the death of Khadija and I was going to make the entire crew responsible pay for her death.

Donnie came home briefly to change his clothes and to pack his luggage. I wanted to pull my weapon right there and kill him but instead I remind quiet. Before he left on his trip I decided to keep track of him by activating his GPS system on his phone. This was so I could locate him with a push of a button. This gave me a great advantage of knowing his exact location.

I despised Chyna and truly needed to get rid of her ass for good. That bitch tryin play games and I wasn't having it. I thought it was time to tell Andrew about what his wifey was truly up to. When we met

HEADGAME   by Brandy

that night I gave him all the pussy he wanted. He tried to fuck my brains out and I let him think he did. I yelled, screamed and pledged that this was his pussy. I even hinted that he was the better man than Donnie.

"Don't you want to be in charge?"

I held him and starting rubbing his chest.

"What?" He replied.

"Don't try to act like you don't know what I mean," I replied rolling over into ball.

"What do you mean?" He asked again.

"I don't fuck with no second class nigga and I thought you was a real gee. You runnin around in this nigga shadow while he was fuckin your girl." I yelled.

"FUCKING Chyna, I don't believe it" He replied. I told him that I just found out about their affair and I showed him the proof that they where together. After I told him what I seen on the cruise ship and he had a bewildered look on his. In his face things started to click and I could tell that things were starting to add up.

"I knew it! I knew it! I always knew it but I turned my head and I really didn't know what to do about the situation. I couldn't bring myself to believe it"

HEADGAME   by Brandy

How could he stand for the shit all this time and not do anything. He later admitted that's why he slept with me and left her. He never thought that he was gonna fall for me but he did. He was whipped by this pussy.

" I love you Vickey. I think I always loved you." He replied as he hugged me.

"I love you too,"

Andrew and I spent the entire weekend together and he made me sick every time I thought of how he did nothing. I was goin to change that and all I needed was time. He talked big shit about killin Donnie but I knew he was no killer. The idea of killing Donnie over some romp with his girl was no excuse but over your wifey was a different story. I attempted to hype up the situation and play upon his ego to spark anger into his heart. I was hoping to encourage him by telling him that if he killed Donnie that he could have it all, including me. The idea of the taking over deeply implanted in his mind and hoped that he played a smart role. I warned him not to let on that we knew of our lover's betrayal. It was important that we concealed our grip for power and not reveal what was goin on between us. Andrew needed to make up with his wife when she returned from my trip. I didn't want Donnie to get suspicious of Andrew or hold anything against him.

HEADGAME   by Brandy

Getting rid of Donnie wouldn't be an easy task and a major player like him had lots of soldiers that remained loyal to him. I wanted him to pay dearly for his deception and his murderous behavior. I needed to step up my game to ensure my victory. I had to prepare for the upcoming funeral of my adopted family.

When Donnie arrived home he was upset at Andrew because he was supposed to make some pick up but failed to do so.

"You need to get yah head out your ass and get that money nigga!" He shouted over the phone. He went on for about 20 minutes and finally got off the phone.

"I don't know what got into this nigga but he fallen off," He said as he hung up the phone.

I could hear Andrew making excuses and pleading his case. He reminded me of the bitchassness that plagued him. It was then that I realized that he didn't have what it takes to be a Don. I would have to force his hand to exact my revenge on him.

"I sorry boss, I sorry"

"I know your ass is sorry," He replied. Donnie was strong willed and once he got something in his head its hard to get it out.

HEADGAME   *by Brandy*

The funeral was closed casket because the twins had made such a mess. The warring between the Philly Cartel and Africans proceeded as usual with Donnie at the helm. Jamal Jr dare not get in is way and succeeded command over to Donnie. It was a dark day for me and watching their bodies lowered into the ground turned to anger. The man I was next to was no longer my love he was my nemesis. I laid my roses over their casket and made a promise that I would have their revenge.

After the funeral Andrew and I met up two times a week. We'd fuck regularly and I plotted my next move. I reminded Andrew over and over that I was ready to be his girl. I would not be ready to give myself to him totally until he was the boss of the Cartel. My headgame must of started to work as Andrew vowed that he would take care of everything but he wasn't foolin me. I knew his scary ass couldn't get up the nerve to make a move. It wasn't long before Donnie and Chyna where goin back outta town and this time they were going to Puerto Rico. This news of there trip to the tropics ate me up inside as I pictured them on the beach kissing and fucking. While they were away I knew that they were laughing at me and I was the butt of her jokes. I was at the end of the road and no longer could go on with my charade. It was the straw that broke camel's back and I decided that I would pull my trigger.

HEADGAME   *by Brandy*

May the chips fall

  I covered my hands with the surgical gloves as I removed the 9mm semi automatic weapon out of the closet with the intent of taking care of business. I was going to exact a harsh revenge on the twins. I screwed the long silencer around its muzzle so I could shoot without being detected and arousing suspicion. It was the perfect time for me to catch up with the twins because they didn't expect that anybody was out hunting for them. I set out to kill the both of them. Since Donnie was out of town

HEADGAME *by Brandy*

and on his trip with his bitch I was going to wait at the Upper Darby stash house because I over heard Donnie telling them to go to there and pick up some money and product. It was there that I would ambush them as they did Jamal and Khadija. I ensured the gun was loaded with one in the chamber giving me eighteen shots. I drove my car as fast as I could to the house and parked a half a block away. I slowly walked to the house and was grateful to have cover of darkness hiding my approach. I didn't see any sign that they had arrived or they where present in the house. I was careful not to smear Donnie finger prints off the weapon, I wanted to ensure that he would be convicted of the of the twins homicides. I arrived at the back door and entered the house with out turning on any lights. In the back room was three suit cases filled with enough cash and drugs to supply the entire east coast. I could have took off with those suit cases and lived very comfortable. I wasn't concerned with money because this was personal and I needed to keep it that way.

I moved the suitcases to the master bedroom where I could hide in the small bathroom. I unscrewed the light bulbs to ensure my dark surprise. I sat on the top step focusing on the front door. Once I heard them parking in the driveway I hid in the bathroom and didn't move. I stayed still and regulated my breathing out my nostrils. It seemed like it was forever until they arrived but finally they came inside the house. The headlight shinning through the window was my signal to await their arrival. I stood in the shower so I couldn't be seen hiding, I waited with the door

HEADGAME by Brandy

cracked open. I could hear them coming closer as their feet pounded onto the wooden floor.

"Man let's go get this money, its in the back room"

"It ain't in here, the fuckin light ain't workin"

"Go check the master bedroom"

"Oh there it is"

I could hear his footstep coming closer as he entered the room. I wasn't sure how I was going to get both of them in the room at the same time. I pulled the gun hammer back so I could ready it to fire. CLINK!

"You heard that"

"Heard what? stop trippin get the bags, Imma take a piss, Aight,"

My eyes widen as he walked toward the bathroom holdin his dick. He placed his weapon on top the sink as he released his water. I slowly reach for his weapon taking it off sink without notice. He looked down to ensure his aim was a good as I pressed the nine millimeter to back of head.

"huh"

I squeezed the trigger signaling a slug to enter into his head. The force of the bullet jerked his body forward and a flash was discharged from the muzzle. What was left of his head slammed into

HEADGAME   *by Brandy*

the mirror and his knees curled over as he slipped down the floor. His body caused a loud thud as the gravity pulled down the dead weight down.

"Hasaan! Hasaan!"

I heard his brother call out as he ran back up the steps. I closed the bathroom door leaving him to bleed out. I quietly changed my position as I maneuvered myself behind the closet. The brother smashed threw the door and ran straight for the bathroom. The bathroom door was not easily opened as his lifeless body slumped against it. He push with all his might but was only able crack open the door. I slipped out the closet and tiptoed behind him. He let out a loud yell as he recognized his brother corpse.

"Who did this to yeah? Who did this to you?

He cried as he leaned over the body crying. I was standing behind him before he recognized my shoe.

"I don't know who you are but you ain't have to kill 'em like dat"

"Well that makes us even. Ya'll didn't have to do Khadija like that, you fuckin bastard"

I squeezed off three shots, two to the head and one in the chest it was over as fast as it started. I placed the smoking weapon on the floor leaving it for the crime scene investigator to find. I search for

HEADGAME   by Brandy

his cell phone and dragged the remaining suitcase through alley into my awaiting car. I dialed 911.

"I wanna report gun shots" at 1411 Mulberry Drive, hurry please somebody dyin"

I hung up the phone and tossed it on the seat as I drive back to my Condo in Center City. I was planning a special nite with Andrew and as usual he was coming to my house for our regular fuck session. On this night I had something different planned for him as I took my long hot shower. I was having second thoughts and doubting if I could set this shit off. While toweling dry my body shook in fear because if this shit didn't go right, there would hell to pay. I slowly wrapped my self in a short satin robe. I pulled my hair back and sat on the couch. The doorbell rang aloud and it was Andrew coming for his serving of me. I let him in so we could play that sex game we play. He chased me around the house and he couldn't keep his paws off the goods. I gulped shots of liquor to provide me with its bravery. I'd already swallowed three shots of henny and I must admit it I was a little tipsy. We rolled around the carpet fooling around and enticing him with my body. After our game of cat and mouse I was brave enough to take him straight to the bedroom. After all my games I never allowed Andrew in the bedroom. Andrew kissed me on my neck, licked around my breast and massaged my ass with his fingers. His tongue searched around my lower stomach and before I knew it I was spread eagle with his tongue licking on my pussy. I moaned and groaned then push his head on my clit. With my other hand I

HEADGAME by Brandy

grabbed the bedroom phone, a private number only Donnie knew. I pushed speed dial and waited for Donnie to pick up the phone. As soon as I heard him say Hello I moaned,

"*ahhh baby eat this pussy*"

I could feel the vibrations of his voice screaming my name.

"*Oooh Andrew you do it so well,*" I purred like a sex kitten over the phone. I threw the phone on the side of bed and let him hear our entire session. I sucked his dick and made the loudest slurps with my mouth. Andrew was squealing for me to suck faster and harder.

"I said say it louder,"

"Please Vickey suck it harder,"he begged.

I let him pound my pussy from the back and I howled like a wolf. I rode him until he was about to cum. I jumped off, slipped the condom of his dick and drank every drop of his cum. He let out a loud yell and collapsed on the bed. I left him breathing and motionless after we finished. I grabbed my phone to see if he was still on the line and he was. I quickly ran out the room and down to the living room.

"Hello," I answered to the phone

"You bitch, you fuckin bitch,"Donnie yelled into the phone.

HEADGAME   by Brandy

"I know you fuckin Chyna! I saw you!,"

"I ain't fuck her, you be trippin," Donnie replied

"That's okay you bastard I found someone to replace your dumbass,

"Who the fuck, who the fuc...," He stuttered as I cut him off with my reply.

"Andrew and I been seein each other for months and I'm havin his baby. He says if you come around us again he's gonna kill your punk ass, I'm leaving with him" I said..

"HE WHAT! TELL THAT MUTHA FUCKA IMMA, KILLYA, III BE ON THE FIRST PLANE BACK AND WHEN.........." Before he could get the rest of his threat out I hung up the phone. I knew he would call the twins and since I had that phone Id had nothing to fear. I had taken care of them and still I was ahead of the game because I had the element of surprise. Donnie called the twins phone and I answered.

"Just in case your looking for the twins, they don't wanna talk to you either, you've been out voted. So long Donnie"

I hung the phone up and thought how nice it was it stayin in this large condominium but it was over and I needed to pack everything of value. I grabbed the black garbage bags as I contemplated

HEADGAME   by Brandy

the task of getting my shit together. My phone continued to ring but I paid it no attention.

I ran up stairs and woke up Andrew.

"Get up nigga! Donnie is on his way! He knows about us and I told him I was havin you're baby,"

Before I got finished this nigga was pale as a ghost and a blank look appeared on his face.

"*You told him what?*" He asked as he seems not to grasp what was going on.

"Well nigga it seems like it is time to ride or die nigga. All that shit you talked its time to back it up."

I tossed his clothes at him. His phone started to ring and he was instantly afraid to answer Donnie's call

"You bitch...You fuckin bitch you been settin me up all this fuckin time," He responded as he balled up his fist and came toward me. The look in his eyes was rage as he threw back his fist. I soon realized that my plan was already back firing and I needed an angle out of this mess.

"The baby! What about the baby?"

I rubbed my stomach signaling I was harnessing a fetus. That nigga didn't hesitate for a minute and slammed his fist into my abdomen as hard as he could. I collapsed to floor trying to regain the air that was knocked out of me.

HEADGAME   by Brandy

"You stupid bitch, I can't have kids I'm sterile," He yelled as he kicked me in the ribs. He turned away to find the rest of his clothes as I crawled out of the room.

"Oh you thought that you was gonna play a mutha fucka," He yelled as he chased behind me. I reached the step and attempted crawl down them. I felt the force of his boot launch me face first down the steps. I rolled to the bottom and blacked out. I awakened with Andrew tying my legs with an extension cord. I reached for the thick crystal ashtray lying next to me. I waited for him to come closer and swung it as hard as I could. "CRACK!" is the sound I heard as blood begun to gush from his forehead. CRACK! CRACK! CRACK! Was sounded as I continued to wallop him across the head. Andrew covered his head and fell to a knee. I jumped on his back and choked him unconscious with the same extension cord that he tried to imprison me with. I cuffed his hands and tied his feet. I lost valuable time fighting with this fool so I needed to get a move on.

That nigga fucked me up and when I looked in the mirror I wanted to cry. The large knot on my forehead was complemented with a black eye and busted lip. My ribs where bruised and my arms where littered with scratches. I got out my luggage and I started to pack all the shit I could carry. I stuffed the jewelry his and mine in the small baggage compartment. The minks, fox, fur coats and shoes where stuffed in the black garbage bag. I already had my stash of cash in the bag. I opened his closet and pulled up the floorboards where he

HEADGAME   *by Brandy*

put several bags of cash and loaded tech nine. I fitted the tech nine in my purse and I stuffed four suitcases full of cash and crammed everything else in the back seat of the car. I sat behind the steering wheel and looked for his GPS his signal but to no avail. I knew he and his whore were probably already on a plane back to Philly. It was only a three hour flight I had to react quickly. I called Margi and told her that I needed her to come right over.

My revenge was not over and I wanted put his ass in jail so he could never hurt anyone again. I knew that Donnie was very careful but I hoped in his haste to get back to the states he would get careless and arrested for smuggling the dope. Eventually he would be charged with murder.

My next phone call was to the United States Customs Agent whose hair I did at the shop. Officer Carole and I had become real cool and I told her that I was gonna need her help with this problem. She picked up the phone after three rings and I was glad that she'd answer

"Hello"

"I gotta a proposition for you, I would you like to report two smugglers coming in from Puerto Rico to Philadelphia International on the 11pm flight. Their names are Donnie Williams and Chyna Santiago and they are smuggling three kilos of Cocaine."

"This sounds personal, what's in it for me"

HEADGAME by Brandy

"five grand"

"Make it ten grand and we gotta deal"

"ten it is, They are comin in tonight"

"then I need my money asap, call me when you get to the parking lot"

"I'm on my way"

After ,I gave her a complete description of them and the promised bounty of ten grand for her assistance in this matter. I decided that I would let the authorities take it from here but I need to drop the money off at the Airport to be assured that he was going to be arrested.

I counted out the ten grand and placed it in my purse. I cleaned my face the best I could and dressed myself. I sat in the living room until Margi drove up to the drive way. I fell into her arms and cried hysterically. I told her that Andrew tried to kill me and he was under orders of Donnie to do it. I fought him off and needed her help with making my escape.

"What happened girl?"

"He tried to kill me"

"Damn girl you sure you ain't kill him. How many times did you hit him with the vase?"

"Oh , about four, five times"

HEADGAME   *by Brandy*

We dragged Andrew into the closet and piled clothes to cover him. I already cuffed his hands but I needed to tie his feet. I didn't want to leave him any room to escape. After I finished subduing him and he started to scream horribly loud. To conceal his screamin I stuffed a pair of my panties into his mouth. I planted the weapon I killed the Twins with under the mattress beside the matching suitcase in the closet. The plan was all set and I was ready for all that happened.

For safety reasons we switched cars. I instructed her to drive to New Jersey to get a motel room on route 38. I wondered how she would act if she knew that she was driving away with over $750,000 in cash and roughly five kilos of dope in the trunk on my car.

HEADGAME   *by Brandy*

Its take two to make things go right

The flight carrying Donnie and his whore was arriving in the next hour. I arranged to meet with the customs officer to make my payoff. This was to ensure that Donnie and his bitch never make it out of the airport. It should only take me thirty minutes to arrive there. I entered the interstate 76 and floored the gas pedal. I hit the airport garage in only twenty minutes and by 10:45 pm I was entering the parking lot at the Philadelphia

HEADGAME   by Brandy

International Airport to meet the plain clothed customs officer.

"Are you sure you can handle this"

"No sweat I got it, you got the money and picture"

"I got it right here"

I pulled ten grand from under my seat and a picture of Donnie and Chyna I acquired on our vacation.

"Its in your hands"

"Don't worry about it were going to get him and if they are carrying drugs like you say they are then they can kiss they asses goodbye"

She folded the money and stuffed it into her jacket as she got out of the car. She disappeared behind the rows of cars as I turned the ignition on. I boldly planned to watch Donnie's demise. I hurried into the airport and searched the arrival screens till I found the 11pm Air Puerto Rico flight arriving @ gate 30. I didn't want to be recognized so I sat in the bar where I could see everyone coming out of the gate. It was a perfect place for me to hide across from the arriving gate. I wondered if my disguise would work or I would be found out. While awaiting the planes arrival some guy sent me a drink.

"Miss the gentleman across the way wants to buy you a drink. What are you having?" The bartender asked.

HEADGAME   by Brandy

I was hesitating and looked over to see if he knew me but he didn't. I smiled and waved so he could come over.

"Ill have shot of Bacardi, no chaser"

I directed him to sit in front me so he could provide me with a cover. I tried to act interested but I hardly noticed him. I kept looking at the arrival television screen then my wrist watch, over and over again.

"My name is Mike," He said as he tried to look into my hidden yes.

"Yeah Mike just move over a little," I said.

I adjusted my hat to cover my face. I quickly thought that I might as well get on a plane if this failed. No one would ever find my dead corpse if my plan didn't work out. I was a dead bitch. My stomach flipped when the screen read that the plane would delay for another half hour. Mike kept trying to get my attention and soon realized that he's being ignored. I finally took time to notice the sexy ass caramel brother sitting before me. His hair was cut short and his platinum chain glitter before my eyes. He had an athletic build that revealed the great god Adonis. . I was stunned at how well he looked and my instant attraction.

"Vickey , my name is Vickey," I said smiling politely.

"Well Vickey I can see you pre occupied maybe when I get back in town we can hook up.," Mike

HEADGAME *by Brandy*

replied as he handed me his card and walked out of the bar. I waited patiently until his plane arrived. I prayed my prayer of courage as the passengers slowly began to trickle off the plane. My breath was still when I saw Donnie walking down the hallway and by his side was the bitch wearing some tacky ass $10 outfit. I wondered what he saw in her, maybe cause the bitch thinkin she was white. I followed slowly and carefully as they walked over to the baggage claim. He picked up their luggage and walked toward the exit. I waited patiently for him to get arrested but nothing happened. I started thinking that officer Carrol had doubled crossed me and took my money. I just knew I was a dead woman as I hug my head low. My eyes begun to form the biggest tears in my life and I started to consider what country I was gonna hide in. I gasp for air as Donnie was immediately surrounded by plain clothes police. He tried to fight them but was thrown to the floor. Chyna knees buckled as they apprehended her standing next to Donnie. Their face expression was highlighted with disgust and disappointment. The officer quickly pulled his hands behind his back and encircled them with steel bracelets. I was delighted when I saw him and that shady bitch arrested. They stood around gathering their belongings. I walk straight toward him, hoping to look him directly in his face. I wanted to make sure he saw me as I passed by him. I took off my hat and glasses so he could see my face. He finally recognized me and coldly looked me in the face. I blew a kiss at him and waved goodbye. This would be my farewell to him because this was the last time he would ever see my black ass again.

HEADGAME by Brandy

"Vickey you bitch, Imma killya Imma killya, "

I switched my ass hard walking away giggling as they dragged Donnie off to be interrogated and searched by the police.

I was proud of myself and happy that I won. I rejoiced in my victory and decided to drive back to the house. I never liked to smoked but this was cause to celebrate as I lit up a victory Cuban cigar. I puffed to fill my mouth with smoke. I made the mistake of inhaling which caused me to cough viciously. I threw the cigar out the window and continued to clear my lungs. I was really feelin myself until I thought of one loose end that needed tieing up. I went back to the house and checked on Andrew. He was kicking the closet door and makin an awful noise. I open the closet, untied his legs and demanded he get out the closet. I marched him to the couch so I could have a heart to heart talk with him. It was still much at stake and he had decision to make. His hands where still handcuffed behind his back and I needed to come to an understanding with him before I set him free. I was hoping we could get through our past and move on to bigger and better things.

"I'm willing forgive you for what you did to me. You see Donnie was picked by the FEDS and I don't think he's gonna make it out anytime soon. The streets need a new Don and it could be you. Donnie's got 10 kilos of coke and hundred thousand cash in the closet upstairs. We can split it

HEADGAME   by Brandy
up and go our separate ways, now node if you agree,"

I waited for his response but he seemed to be weighing the pros and cons of the situation. At first he shook his head slowly in agreement with our deal. I pulled the panties from his mouth.

"Aight Vickey just uncuff me please"

"Do we have an understanding?"

"Yeah sure we can split the money and the dope"

"I glad to see that we got a deal"

I uncuffed his hand and allowed him to move about freely. He tossed the cuff onto the floor leaving his hands open. I turned my back to walk away and before I got three steps his hands grabbed me around my throat.

"I thought we had an agreement,"

"Fuck you Vickey, Imma kill ya and take all the fuckin money and the dope," He called as he continued his attack against me. I reached in my purse and pulled the tech nine and pressed it against his chest. BRRRRRT! BRRRRT! BRRRRRT! The bullets sounded as it left the chamber and slammed into his chest. The sparks from the muzzle had set his shirt on fire as his body dropped to the floor. He gasped for air while holding his chest. The blood spattered on me causing me to have little blood dots across my

HEADGAME by Brandy

face. I wiped the warm blood from my face and neck. I became nausea at the smell of burnt flesh. It was my third kill of the night and I was having no remorse for the lives I've taken. I believed in what I was doing and remorse is for the weak. I had no time for self pity.

"*Bitch you betta your ass together, get your shit together,*" I repeated to myself. Dragged the suitcase from Upper Darby that contained the dope and cash. I laid it next him with the Twins cell phone. I had taken the money and drugs Donnie had out of the house earlier. Poor stupid Andrew lay dead and I felt a little bad for him. But since he wanted to be greedy, fuck him and the horse he rode in on. He beat me so badly that my eye was closing and my stomach had a large bruise. I stumbled over to the refrigerator and searched for the ice tray so I could put ice on my wound. With all that was going on my adrenaline was pumping and I didn't feel any pain. It was hard for me to breathe as I took in deep breath. I searched the refrigerator for a vial of Andrew's sperm that I collected. He thought I was letting him cum in my mouth for his pleasure. I was collecting and storing it for just such an occasion. I poured the substance in between my ass crack and rubbed in my vagina. With what was left in the vial I put on my panties that where torn off. To give more dramatic appeal I ripped my shirt open and laid on the floor. I dialed 911 and awaited the police and ambulance arrival. They where on the scene in five minutes.

"I'm in here! I'm in here!" I cried as the tall dark officer came to my rescue.

HEADGAME by Brandy

"He hurt me, He hurt me"

"Don't worry we gotya"

"He raped He raped"

It was easy for me to act like I was traumatized and upset while I had the attention of the strong officer. I grabbed on to him giving him the impression that he was my savior. He obliged and held me tightly. I cried hysterically as I watched the home quickly fill up with officers and paramedics. They attempted to revive Andrew but that was in vain. He was pronounced death on site as they attempted chest compressions. His heart failed to show vital signs as he lay dead. I was placed on the stretcher, strapped in and carried to the awaiting ambulance. The sirens blared as the truck raced to the emergency room. I kept up my role as traumatized patient as I now lay on the gurney curled into a ball.

At the hospital I had to submit to a rape kit and a total examination. They poked at me, took pictures and stuck a large swabb inside my pussy. They asked for urine a sample and for me to take an x-ray. The x-ray showed that I had a fracture jaw and cracked ribs. My arms was bruised and wrapped in a sling. I needed stitches to sew up my head and large bandage to soothe my concussion. I was given a sedative to relax and that's when the detective appeared for my statement.

HEADGAME   by Brandy

I told them that Andrew was a friend of the family and he came over looking for my brother. I told him he wasn't here and he pushes me aside. All of sudden he was threatening me with gun. He made me undress, attacked me and pinned me down. I was so frightened for my life," as I cried.

"So what do you know about Donnie Williams"

"That is my boyfriend is he okay"

"He's just fine? Are you familiar with what type of work he is in"

"Real estate, he told me real estate"

"What do you know Rasaan and Hassan Tibbel?"

"They are handy man that work for Donnie"

"Are you aware of a red suitcase?"

"The suitcase that Andrew brought over"

I answered all the detectives' questions to the best of my abilities and I could tell that I was pissing him off. He sucked his teeth and slammed his hand together. Once he decided I was no help to him he concluded the interview.

After my interview was over I called Margi and told her to come to the hospital I was officially released.

HEADGAME   by Brandy

The police stated they would be in touch with me. I went home with Margi and she started askin a lot of questions.

"How did Andrew get out the closet?" She asked

"I let him out and he attacked me,"

"So have you heard from Donnie?,"

"I ain't heard shit,"

"Well, just to let you know he was arrested at the airport with Chyna," She blurted out.

"Arrested by Why? I'm tired," I responded by closing my eyes and visualizing all the money and dope I stashed away.

"Cutoms got em, that's all I heard about"

"Oh okay"

"Is that all you can say oh, I just told you your fiancé is locked"

"We are no longer engaged beside he tried to kill me or did you forgot"

"Do you really believe that he would do that?"

"Yes I believe it and what the fuck are you? A cop or somethin"

"All I'm sayin is...."

HEADGAME   by Brandy

"Mind your business"

"Oh its like that now"

"What ever Margi I don't like how you're questioning me"

I sat silent as we drove to the hotel on the New Jersey route 38. All I needed was some rest because it had been the longest night of my life. I thought about the twins and how I ambushed them in the bathroom with my 9mm silencer. I pictured their body jerking as the slugs entered them. I recalled Donnie yelling when he heard Andrew and I fucking. The disgusted look he had in his eyes as the police escorted him away. I then remembered fucking Andrew, enduring his ass wiping and then killing him. I survived it although I was beaten and bruised. I was victorious and how I would reap the rewards. I was rich and I finally made it to the top. It was going to be along road to recovery but I will make it. When I entered the hotel room it was sleazy and dirty. Any other time I would have packed my shit and ran to another hotel but this time I fell into the pillow. My knees collapsed over the bed as I lay on my stomach. The pressure hurt my ribs as I rolled over on my back. My eyelids closed and I drifted off to sleep. How was I to know this was the last time I was able to rest in peace.

HEADGAME by Brandy

Big Timer

I woke up early that morning as the suns rays shined over the bed. On my way to bathroom I scared the roaches as I flipped the light switch on. I mashed a roach with my bare feet causing its innards to get stuck on the bottom. I sat on the toilet bowl to do my business. I swung my towel to scare them away but they refused to run. I emptied my bladder and noticed blood my urine. This must've come from the fight I had. I swallowed some pain killers so I could move around without feeling that much pain. I turned the shower on and had to wait five minutes before the water to reach steaming hot. I took off my clothes, pulled the hospital tag off my arm and stepped into the hot water. I left the water run down my body as it soothed my pain. I stayed in the shower until the water was no longer hot enough for my licking. I dried my skin with a towel and looked through my bags for something to wear. I was sore from last night adventure but it was a load lifted off my chest.

I packed everything I had into the trunk of my car. I was planning a special trip, I'd promised God if I

HEADGAME *by Brandy*

got though this I was going to go see my mother. It had been so long since I've seen her or checked on her. I finally admitted to myself that I was ashamed of her and hated her for dropping out on me. If she was here I would have never stoop to the lows I had too. Since going though my own drama and circumstances I know understood her plight. I grew up fast and hard the past couple of months. I received a new respect for my mom because she fought for me all her life. I needed to tell her thank you and to show her some love. I wanted be forgiven for my neglect of her. I thought of making this trip to the institution several times but I always canceled for some reason or other. I wanted to see my mother but hated the crazed looks in her eye. She'd stare out in the distance with no movement or correspondence.

It was a thirty minute ride to the Suncrest Mental Institution in Westchester PA. I didn't tune into the radio as I drove on the roadway. All I thought about is my next move and what I was going to do.

I counted seven hundred thousand dollars and five kilo's of heroin from Donnie's stash. I thought of making a new start with all that money but I wanted to sell the five kilos of dope to somebody outside the Cartel. It was only one person that I could rely on to find a buyer and that was Carmen. We last crossed paths at the funeral home and I told her that I would be stopping by her house soon. I knew Carmen could help me find a buyer with no problem. I wanted to move fast because there was going to be a lot of questions and I didn't want to have to answer them. Donnie still had a lot

HEADGAME   *by Brandy*

of clout on the streets and could arrange a hit on me with no problem.

I drove past the large gate which enclosed the entire hospital grounds. The windows where barred and doors where covered with steel mass trapping the sun light in. I hated going to this place but it was the trip that I needed to make. I signed in and the burly nurse escorted me down a long hallway to her room. When I saw her I hardly recognized her, she was so skinny that her cheeks bones were sticking out of her skin. Her face was hardened with lines of stress. She had a hard life and I could see it though her eyes. I reached out and hugged her tightly.

"Hi mommy! I came to see. How you whoro doin?"

I thought I saw her smile when she saw me. I squeezed the breath out of her and she pulled away grasping holding her shoulder in pain. She jumped when I touched her shoulder. I pulled her shirt up and it revealed a large bruise on her back. When I saw that I lost it completely and started cussing the people in the facility.

"What the fuck y'all do to muva? Ya'll sons of bitches in here hurtin momma" I ranted until I was threatened that the police would be called and I'd be removed from the property. Considering all the drugs and money I had in my car I calmed down quickly. I asked to meet with the administrator to disscus my moms injury. The administration gave

HEADGAME   by Brandy

me a bullshit story about how she had fallen to the ground. His arrogant persona rubbed me the wrong way as he handed me a stack of brochures to private nursing facilities.

"I'm sad that your mother fell and she has been very hard to get along with."

"How did she fall?"

He handed me the report which I could barely read. He then gave me a long speech about Medicare, his patient ratio and lack of staff. He argued that my mother was getting older and would require a lot more care and was doubtful about being able to handle her needs. I was must upset at myself for not coming to see her in such a long time. I was ashamed and promised that I would make it right. I slowly walked back to her room. She didn't say a word to me but I knew I had to do something quick. I decided that I would make her more comfortable and began read through the brochures of nursing homes. The Woody Crest nursing seemed like a beautiful place she would have a private room, her own nurse and the best medical care. The elderly people looked so healthy and full of life. I wanted to do that for her and this was the least I could do for her. I wished that she could stay with me and Id take care of her but that was a dream wrapped up in some other shit.

The nursing home would cost six thousand month which totaled seventy two thousand dollars a year.

HEADGAME   by Brandy

When I added up the figures and realized that if I did that I would be broke with in a couple years. I still had my life style to maintain and so desperately wanted to keep it up. I was in a somber mood when I walked out the facility and realized that my journey has just begun. All I could think of was getting my mother to a better place. I went back to my car and counted fifty thousand dollars. I marched straight to the administrators office and tossed the money on the table.

"That should take care of her for awhile; I want you to make sure she has everything she needs"

"Ms Diamond I'm afraid I can't take your money"

"I did ask you what you're afraid of, Listen take care of my mom and there's more where that came from"

"I understand"

"I need you to prepare her transfer and for know she needs a private room"

"Is there any thing else you require Ms Diamond"

"Yeah, Fire the bitch that let my momma fall"

"no problem"

Once I gave him the money his demeanor was much more pleasant. He seemed happier that we can up with such an agreement. I needed more money and the only plan that seems to make

HEADGAME   by Brandy

sense was to go see Carmen and let her see if she could help sell the five kilos of heroin. It wouldn't be difficult for her to sell the weight with her contacts in the business. She cooks up for so many players that she wouldn't have a problem. I didn't know the first thing about selling dope but I was interested in finding out. Sitting around Donnie I used hear him talking about weight and quality of the work. He would say its" pure" or "uncut", every time he talked to his dealers. When he talked with Carmen he tells her to put a three or a four on it and I assumed he meant the amount of cut. I did know that Donnie dope was pure and strong. I could command any price I wanted for his product. I needed to keep the dope in cool place so it wouldn't fall. Donnie used to lose his mind when found out the dope fell. He warned them to keep it in a shoe box covered with rice. He said the rice took away the moisture.

I drove down the freeway back into the familiarity of the Philadelphian City. The traffic on Girard Ave moved so slow that I grew impatient to get by. I drove past the trolley almost crashing into side of it and ran though the red light. I slowly drove up her the block hoping to see if she was standing on the porch, but that wasn't my luck today. I parked the car and walked to the door. Inhaled deeply *"Knock! knock! knock!* sounded the door. It wasn't long before she opened the door and comforted me with her warm welcome.

HEADGAME   by Brandy

"Is dat my baby Pooke Dooke," she sounded off as she grabbed me around the neck and hugged me tightly.

"Hey mama, " I calmly let out as I felt her warm body press against mine. I was just as excited to see her that I didn't mind her calling me that silly ole name.

"Oh I heard what happened to Donnie and Andrew are you okay sweetie," She asked me. I told her that Andrew tried to kill me and I was trying to get money for Donnie's lawyer.

"Oh," she replied as she continued to smoke on her cigarette. I wondered if Donnie put out the word that i snitched on him and his bitch.

"Did you hear from him," She asked.

"ahh he just called and told me to come to you so we could handle his business for him," I replied shifting the questions to something.

" I will do all I can for ya'll"

"Good cause I got some product that need movin"

"whatya got "

"Five kilos of dope"

"DAMN FIVE KEYS, that a tell order"

"Can u do it?"

HEADGAME   *by Brandy*

"It 'll take couple of days but I can do it . When is his bail hearing? "

I hesitated for a moment because I forgot about that bail shit. I didn't plan for that and anyway I had all is money. He couldn't make bail at least I hoped he couldn't. I cried hard so I could show her how upset I really was and she wrapped me in her arms to hold me tight.

"I missed him so much"

"I know sugar, I know"

"I can't wait till he comes home,"

I then told her that we were in a tight squeeze and we needed cash. I told her the feds raided the house and confiscated what money he left me. All the cash to take care of the house was tied up in the killos. My survival depended on how fast I could sell this product. I would leave it to Carmen to me to make it happen. It ways only through her connections that we had a chance to move all that weight. I told her I was afraid for my life and in hiding. I asked her what it was worth on the street. She heard a kilo of dope was going for one hundred thousand a piece or more - depending on the quality. I got a half million dollars of dope and I was riding it around in the trunk of my car. My mouth went dry and my body started to sweat at the idea of making that much money. I didn't want to admit it to her but it was sounding very appealing to me.

HEADGAME   by Brandy

"Fuck five hundred thousand dollars, I can use that. She even hinted that with Donnie gone there is a void in the streets and if we broke it down we could make at least 1.5 million dollars. I thought long and hard but I wasn't feelin that waiting around. I wanted a lump sum of cash so I could dissapear and be comfortable.

"Are you sure that you can find a buyer for all this shit,

"I gotta a few connections that may interest but there is a ten percent finder fee," she added as she looked me up and sown.

"Shit Pooke dooke that's a lot of dope. Do you have really that much to get rid of? Where is it at? Do you have it now?" She kept firing off questions like she was the FBI interrogator.

"It's in a safe place, all I gotta do is get it," She could tell that I was not feelin all the questions. I was reluctant to answer her because it was none of her business.

"Listen Vickey I can set you up with a crew that can sell this shit, I can mix it and bag it up for you, I'm sorry for all questions but with all that shit we can blow these niggas mind" Carmen replied as she rubbed her fingers together. The piercing stare she gave me made me worried. I now grasped why Donnie was so paranoid. It was because when people started talking about money they changed for the worst

HEADGAME   by Brandy

"I don't know nothin about this dope game and I really don't want no part of it."

I shook my head in worry that I would get takin off like I did when I tried to sell weed back in the day. But this was a new day and my survival depended on it. I was not goin to be ripped off because I was willing to die over my money. I would protect my dope at all cost even if it meant killing those who challenged me. My greed was starting to get the best of me.

"I can make it so you ain't gotta do nothin but sit back and collect the dough," Carmen said.

She was trying to convince me that I should put the dope on the streets. I wouldn't consider such a dangerous move. I pleaded with her to find a wholesale buyer for my dope. She was persistent on persuading me to bag it and sell it myself but I was not having it. Even though she still didn't agree with me she finally did as I asked. For a moment I wondered if I should of trusted her but in reality I knew out of all the people in this world I could trust Carmen. She was like a mother to me and would never betray me. I didn't want think about all the money I could collect off those kilos of dope. I didn't want to let her know that her proposition of collecting 1.5 million sounded like music to my ears. That type of money appealed to my greedy side. The thoughts of having that kind of money made my pussy dripping wet. I shivered inside when I thought about the greater good I could do with a million and a half dollars.

HEADGAME *by Brandy*

Let's make a deal

HEADGAME   by Brandy

It took Carmen three days to find a buyer and I was a little apprehensive about the situation. The meeting was planned for the end of the week and I needed time to prepare. I wasn't playing for nickel and dimes. I was playin a big boy game and wasn't going to under estimate the powers that be. I'm not going to allow myself to be caught off guard. I decided I needed to spice thing up and go see my homie Jamal on 60th and Market Street. He sits on the boulevard right outside TONY Boys. While I waited for Jamal I ordered one of their famous cheese steaks platters. I watched the heavy drug trafficking in the area. Shit was really goin down as I watched the hands quickly exchange product for money. It was like a pharmacy for sale out there with all the drugs your hearts desired; xanies, percocets, morphine, dope and crack. The counter lady called out my initials as she wrapped the platter to go. I lounged for another fifthteen minutes and waited for Jamal to arrive at his normal hang out. He was a short and with large belly that covered his legs. He wobbled when he work but he was a deadly man. I knew he would be surprised to see me sitting in the dinner. When he recognized me through the glass window he ran inside the building and gave me a hug like never before.

"Vickey sup"

"Just coolin and it look like you loosin weight"

"Yeah baby don't tell anybody... I heard about Donnie and Twins....dats wild yo... FUCK WHAT HAPPENED TO YOUR FACE"

HEADGAME   by Brandy

"I walked into a door...but seriously thats what I'm here for I gotta protect myself"

"Whatya need.. Anything just say it"

"I need some heat something with some pop on it and something I can conceal"

"I got just the thing for you"

He left the restaurant, returned 10 minutes later and handed me a nine-millimeter and a small caliber 32 automatic.

I handed him "*a grand*" and thanked him for his time. He want to continue chit chatting but I kept it moving. Something in the pit of my stomach was tellin me that something was going on. I reassured myself that shit was gonna be alright and I had nothing to worry about. I blamed my fear on the sudden paranoia I was feeling. I kept looking out of the rare view mirror as if someone was following me. I closed my eyes and took a deep breathe.

"Hold it together, Hold it together"

It was days until the meeting was scheduled and I wasn't feeling safe at Margi's home. The couple of days I had wait for the meeting I decided to go completely underground. While driving home I circled the block three time to ensure I wasn't being followed. I parked by the salon to checked up on things from a distance. I didn't want to go inside because I didn't want anyone to know I was around. I could see the girls getting their hair

HEADGAME   by Brandy

done. Margi had moved her chair toward the front door so she could be closer to the front. I don't know if she saw me as I watched the people tending to their business. I missed hangin at the shop and doin my own thing. That life I once knew was gone because I had crossed the line. Like it or not I was an outlaw living on the edge of society. It was a lonely game but my isolation would be over as soon as I flipped those bricks.

My last couple of days where spent at Margi house but since I got the call from Carmen it was time for me to leave from there. While she was at work I packed my belongings into the car. It wasn't safe for her because if anyone found out that I was living here. She could get killed and I didn't want anybody else to die because of my mess. I hadn't been totally honest with her and now I had sneak out of Margi's house in the middle of the day. I hoped that she didn't take it personal but she will be thankful later.

Margi made me nervous at times with her constant questioning and meddling into my business. I knew she had my back but if things got rough I didn't want her involved. I would temporarily stay at a small furnished apartment I found in Southwest Philly. I rented it from an elderly women who didn't ask much and her only question was if I could pay. I hated the little place but it came with a garage attached. I bought a new fully loaded black Cadillac Escalade with tinted windows. This was the vehicle I was preparing for my get away with. I already stashed most of the cash inside the backseat. I painstakingly pulled out the seats and

HEADGAME   *by Brandy*

duck taped the money to the back of them. This was a little trick I learned from Donnie. The money was well hidden and ready to be transported. It was feat to conceal $750, OOO in that truck, but I did it. When finished with this meeting I was gonna get outta town quickly. The sound of a million dollar had a nice ring to it and that would be my seed money. A million in cash - what a way to start off my new life.

Finally the night of the deal came and I still was apprehensive of the whole thing. I had time to think things through and this was the best solution. It was 7pm and I needed to get ready for the drop off. I changed into a mini dress, halter top and stilettos. I tucked the nine in the back of my waste and 32 automatic I stuck inside my inner thigh letting the garter belt hold it in place. It was uncomfortable as it rubbed against my inner leg. I was excited and horrified all at the same time. I was hyped when it was time to go. I wrapped myself in my full length mink coat. I stopped to look in the rearview mirror and I noticed the swelling had subsided. I eased on my lip-gloss and shaded my cheeks with blush. I wanted to be prepared for whatever happened. I never been to a drug deal before and I didn't want them to think that I wasn't about my business. I exhaled as I started the engine and drove to Carmen's house. As I arrived in front of her house there was no movement. The buyers hadn't arrived yet and I needed to prepare for the delivery. I picked up the oversized Gucci Bag containing the bricks of cocaine. I walk toward slowly to the door searching for anything out of place. By the time my legs

HEADGAME by Brandy

reached the first step leading to the porch Carmen was opening the door. I moved passed her without saying a word and walking into the dining room. She closed the behind me and inquire what I had in my bag.

"Do u have it?" she asked.

"Yeah it's in the bag," I replied as I stopped to look around the room.

"How well do you know these buyers?" I asked as I nervously chewed on the side of my lips.

"They work for the Africans and looking for some weight. You don't have anything to worry about it." She remarked trying to put my inpatients to rest. We sat at the table for nearly an hour and they didnt show for the appiontment. I was tired of waiting and growing very impatient.

"Well fuck then, I'm outta here," I said as I grabbed the bag step to the door. When I got to the door a crème colored Ford Explorer parked in front of the house and out stepped two gentlemen wearing darks suits, shades and carrying a breifcase.

"That's them," she remarked as she pulled me into the house. The two men soon walked into the house watching every move and looking completely paranoid. They talked with a strong accent making understanding them very difficult.

HEADGAME *by Brandy*

"OK Carmen we don't hava all for the day, do hava da shitee, where is da the stuff?," The tall slender gentleman asked

"Right here, she got it right here," Carmen answered. She nudges me to put dope on the table. I complied with the request as they cut open the package and begun to testing the potency of the drug.

"OH SHEET Dis Mudda fucka is spure! It is 90 persent spure heroin" The slender man shouted as he snorted a small portion and tasted it on his tongue. His nose burned as the pure heroin took a hold on him. I watched him as he reached for the rest of the dope with out showing me any money. I got nervous from that bullshit so I quickly closed the bag over his arms.

"Ok where's my money?" I asked as I stood between him and my dope.

"We hava u mommy, rite dear, its all right deer," He said as handed me the briefcase. I unzipped the bag and my eyes were dazzled by all the cash that lay before me. I was hypnotized by all that money in my presence. I was staring at the money when I noticed him checkin me out with his evil looking eyes. I was ready to react on any wrong move he made .

"Carmen count this shit," I ordered. I handed her the brief case and I moved out of her way. It seemed like this shit was taking forever as the counting and testing went on. I held my breathe as

HEADGAME by Brandy

all this went on, the silence was menacing and I knew this was not a game. The two men put my dope in their bag and tried to walk out.

"Hold on motha fucka. You ain't goin no where wit my shit until I count the money," I said. I stood in between them and the door blocking their exit.

"Carmen you hurre and betta get dis bitch. She make big problem for you, she not know who she fucka wit," The smaller man warned as he put his hand in his jacket. Before he blinked I drew my nine millimeter.

"Whoa! Whoa!," The slender man yelled as he motioned for his partner to holster his piece.

"Yo man put dat shit up! dis no ain't time for is John Wayne bullshit." He said as he waved his hand. He put his piece into his holster as I tucked the nine into my waist.

"Got damnit man you ain't not gotta be like dat," he said as the look of anger and frustration was beaming from his eyes. I didn't blink or move a muscle. I wanted him to see that I was not scared of him and his little gun.

"First of all I ain't yo mamma and second if y'all pull the gun shit again we gonna be some shootin mutha fucka in here," I said as I screwed my face evil as possible. The room fell silent as my challenged seem to echo off the walls of the house.

HEADGAME by Brandy

"Its only two hundred fifty thousand dollars in here. Where is the rest?" Carmen asked she looked me in the eye.

"Oh we lefta dee rest of money in de car," The tall one said as he smiled politely.

"The deal was five hundred, not two hundred, "I asked as I rubbed my chin.

"Com on takey de monee we gibben to you," he said as he again tried to walk out the door. I step in his way to block his exit but he forcefully pushed me back. I lost my balance and as I fell back, both of the men started reaching inside their jackets. To answer their move I attempted to reached for my piece but it was to late. Pop! Pop! Pop! Sounded as the slugs came flying toward me. I could feel the force of the bullets as it pass throw the large fur coat. I was sure that I was mortally wounded by the time I landed on the floor. The smaller man aimed at Carmen and unloaded a full clip into her body. As the bullets entered her it caused her to jerk violently off the floor. I clinched the weapon in my hand and attempted to point it at him. That's when I was met with his foot that kicked it out my hand. The gun disappeared under the couch and now I lay on the ground defenseless. My body was sprawled out across the floor and I truly thought I was bleeding to death. The taller man stood over me and aimed the barrel of his gun for my face. I adjusted my body into a fetal position bracing for the bullets impact, that's when I heard the loud a "Click," signaling the bullet misfired or jammed in

HEADGAME by Brandy

the clip. I remembered the 32 semi auto between my thighs and reached for it.

"Yo maybe we taka dat poosy and git a taste of dis fine American poosy before we finicha dis bitch off," He added as he turned away to talk to his friend and pulled back chamber flinging the jammed bullet out of the barrel.

"Oh dat's som good american poosy dere but I hear she sucka dick betta den de supa head," He replied to his friend as they let out a loud laugh. I removed the pistol as he talked and pointed to his chest. Blocka! Blocka! The small caliber sounded as one slung entered his chest and the other slammed into his forehead instantly killing him. I rolled over , just messing his falling body. I shot two more times aiming for the smaller mans stoutly legs.

"Ahhhh!" The man shouted as his legs gave way from the force of the bullets. The rest of his body hit the wall and slid down to the floor. He pointed his weapon and squeezed the trigger forgetting he didn't reload. I held both hands on my weapon aiming for the center of his chest. I sent my last three bullets toward him. The first bullet missed but the second and third hit the mark. His chest jerked and blood spilled from his mouth as he gasped his last sips of air. I still thought I was shot as I ran my hand across my body checking for wounds.

"Holly shit!" Im still alive! I'm still alive! I shouted. I crawled to Carmen but it was two late for her. I helplessly watched her bleed to death. She made a

HEADGAME   *by Brandy*

couple of gargling noises but her pulse faded rapidly. Her body went limp as her life force left her body.

"Oh Damn Momma, Not you...Why you"

I cried out loudly as I rocked her back and forth. I didn't pay attention to the blood dripping out of her dead body. Her eyes were open like she was looking at me. I soon realized that I needed to leave her before the authorities arrived. I went to the kitchen to get some garbage bags and when I returned the wounded African was scratching at the front door. The African managed to crawl over to the door and tried to escape. I ran over to him and kicked him as hard as I could. He moaned in pain as my foot was rammed into his side. He was alive but I wanted to end his suffering quietly. I grabbed the large fluffy sofa pillow and covered his face. I held it there until I was sure he was dead. He tried to kick out of the pillow but he was to weak. I suffocated him and he was dead with in minutes. I gathered the money, drugs and escaped to my car.

HEADGAME *by Brandy*

Death of the Maiden

HEADGAME   by Brandy

I was emotionally destroyed by guilt over the violent death of Carmen. Witnessing her tragic passing was eating me alive. The dark circles were wrapped around my eyes as a good night sleep avoided me. I had lost the only person I truly trusted and always depended on her to kick my ass when I needed it most. She was like a mother to me and now she was gone. It felt as if I was cursed as the spirit of love avoided me. I had nightmares of seeing her shot over and over again. Her face expression of when the bullets entered her body haunted me. I cried my eyes out for my lost. Some nights I'd woke up drenched in sweat and that's when I was able to sleep. On most nights I just lay awake looking up at the ceiling. I contemplated taking some sleeping pills but I was frightened Id never wakes up. I dreaded going to her funeral as the days came near. Making excuses and finding reasons not to go was all I thought of but Margi encouraged my attending.

The large funeral home was upscale and decorated with black and red textile on the wall. The glowing red carpet swept across floor from end to end. I paid for her funeral and the wake but Margi handled all the arrangements. She ordered the finest casket they had to offer. The custom decorated flowers cost me three thousand dollars. I had her mother flown in from Atlanta GA. At the funeral no expense was sparred. The limousines filled the entire block as neighbors crowded into the church to hear the famous R&B singer from Philly sing her favorite tunes. It was a long day and

HEADGAME by Brandy

I felt like I sent her off the best I could. At the end of the funeral I took a minute alone with her. I knelt in front of her and begged for forgiveness. I never meant for her to get killed. She looked so peaceful that I swore she was sleep. I broke down and cried for the passing of my friend. It was then Margi cornered me at my weakest moment yet. I confessed all: that I slept with Andrew because Donnie slept with his wife. I really wanted to get him back for his betrayal. I took his money and dope. I lied to Andrew about being pregnant and I tried to make deal with him but he tried to strangle me. I killed him and made it look like a rape. I snitched on Chyna and Donnie about the drugs they were carrying. I also told her how Carmen died helping me sell Donnie's drugs and the two men I murdered in the process. She looked confused as she folded her arms and listened intently. I cried for all I went through and I just needed her to understand my plight. She sat quietly and nodded her head. I could tell that she was playing it all out in and calculating what I told her.

"Damn Vickey you could of told me about this shit sooner, I would of had your back, no matter what," Margi said as she rolled her eyes at me. Her body language became defiant as I describe my deeds to her.

"Let me make it up to you," I begged her. After all she was the only friend I had left and I wanted at least do right by her.

HEADGAME   by Brandy

"Fuck you Vickey you got me caught in your murderess lies," She shouted. Her insult stung but I understood her anger toward me. She stood to her feet and stepped toward the door.

"I know what I done is horrible and your probably don't wanna be my friend anymore," I said as I reached in my bag and pulled out the deed to my building.

"Your right Vickey... What you did is horrible and unforgivable. I could have been killed"

" I'm so sorry for that but I'm goin away for a while and I want you to have the building, I'm gonna sign it over to you as gift for being my friend. Hopefully, I can make it up to you" I said as I reached out for a hug.

" Your giving me the building , so the shops are mine?" she asked trying to clarify my gesture.

"Yes Margi everything," I replied as I signed my name on the transfer paper. I handed her seventy five thousands dollar in manila envelope. I know this would be the last time that I would see her. We both knew that Donnie would kill me by any means necessary. She warned me of the power and the large crew he controlled. I wasn't stupid at all and I knew that I could be hunted. She wasn't tellin me anything that I didn't know. I knew that it was time to move. After we cried together I said my good byes to my friend. I told her that I was going to Baltimore to visit some family. I hated that I told her another lie but I needed to mislead her , so I could

HEADGAME   *by Brandy*

get her off my scent. I had been planning a new start for so long and a new day would be today.

It was goods news to my ears that Donnie was denied bail and retained until his trial date. The ambitious District Attorney charged him with drug trafficking and conspiracy to internationally drug trafficking. His sentence carried 30 years and it was a relief to know that he wasn't getting out anytime soon. The Twins bodies had been found and he was also being charged with two counts of murder in the first degree. He was looking at a death sentence if convicted on first degree murder charges. The courts deemed him such a threat he could have no contact with the outside world. He was only allowed to speak to his lawyer. The solitary confinement he would have to endure for 23 hours a day would challenge any man. He was destroyed and broken. I felt no remorse for what transpired and only wished I could do more.

Jamal Jr took over for the Philly Cartel and sent word that he needed to meet with me. I was hesitant to agree with such a meeting but I felt he was owed an explanation. I had made it my business to seek and destroy my enemies. I lacked the time to make alliances or allow anyone to see my moves. Even though Jamal Jr lacked the viciousness and control over the Cartel like his father he was not to be under estimated. Jamal jr waited for me outside the funeral home inside the stretched limousine. He was surrounded by arm body guards and anyone that came close to the

HEADGAME   *by Brandy*

car was immediately searched. Even I the family closet friend had to relinquish my weapons. I sat in the wide bodied limousine looking directly at Jamal Jr. His face was hard and his dark complexion shined. He removed his glasses and I could see the new crime boss was vexed. I hoped his anger was not directed at me.

"JJ Howya doin"

"Vickey.. ur a hard girl to track down these days"

"I've been very busy"

"I've heard how busy you've been"

"Aight JJ let's cut out the formalities. What sup? I know you aint come here to chit chat"

"Donnie has met with an unsuspecting incarceration and his lawyer reports you are an informant"

"Donnie was responsible for the hit on your mom and dad. He paid the twin's 50,000 a piece to do the hit. Donnie also had his sight on taking over the Cartel. I loved your parents as if they were my own. I had to do something to stop him"

"I appreciate your help in the matter but are an Informant?"

"No I am not"

HEADGAME   by Brandy

"Why should I believe you? You could be informing on the family"

"Do you really believe that?"

"I don't believe it and I knew that snake had somethin to do with my parent's murder. I appreciate what you have done for the organization and I'm in your debt.. So for your loyalty to my parents I'm gonna give you some information because your in grave danger"

"Why? What is going on?

"My Dad and Mom loved you and I always seen you as my sister. The word is about you bein a snitch and it is not safe for you in Philly. He put a $100,000 contract out on your life and every shooter in Philly we be lookin for you."

"I got some business to attend to then I'm going on a little vacation"

"You need to get out of town asap.. I can't protect you with that type price on your head"

"I know I have got to go"

"Vickey you know I'm supposed to kill you for informing on any associate of the cartel. That is rule number one right after stealing"

"I know"

HEADGAME   by Brandy

"But being this is personal and not business I inclined to look away. However if we cross paths in the future I might have to handle it differently"

"Thanx!"

I hugged him and stepped out of the limo. I thought I was a goner but this meeting reinforced all the fears that I was having. Jamal needed to save face and needed to show his strength. He may have wanted to kill me since I was the closet person to Donnie.

The detective deemed the Andrew shooting as self defense and no charges were ever filed against me. I made my way to the police plaza to give my written statement. My lawyer showed at $500 dollars hour rate. I wrote down my statement and the Detectives questioned for another two hours. They kept asking me to recall what happened. I stuck to my story and told it the same way over and over again. They tried to get me to slip up and make mistakes. They even swore that Andrew was still alive and he fingered me. I told them he was a liar and didn't know the truth unless it slapped him across the face. I stuck to my guns and when I finally got feed up with their fishing expedition. I looked to my lawyer to get me outta here as soon as possible.

"My client is tired of answering the same question. Is she being arrested?" The lawyer asked as fell back into the chair folding his hand behind her head.

HEADGAME   *by Brandy*

"No , she not being arrest as of now," The detective replied as he folded his hands and stared at me.

"Well are you filing formal charges against her?

"No, we have no evidence"

"Well since she's not under arrest and has cooperated with you to highest extent then we will be leaving, I advise you not harass my client and if you have any further question please contact me " He replied as he slowly stood up, handed them his business card and escorted me to the door. I hurried out the station and thanked my lawyer for his support on this matter. I handed him an enveloped containing five grand.

"This for your retainer fee and it has two grand more than we agreed. I'm goin on a vacation and I need you keep up with this shit. I'm gonna keep the same number so you can contact me if you need too," I said.

"Ms. Diamond you're so generous"

He snatched the envelope and stuffed it inside his jacket. He smiled at me as he watches me fade out into the darkness. I walked quickly to my car and drove away hoping to never see this place again. I was ready to disappear and made up my mind to go Coney Island section of Brooklyn New York. My crazy ass cousin Jessie lives there. We speak on the phone frequently and she had invited me many times to come visit her. I used to make excuses

HEADGAME   by Brandy

about why I didn't spend the night with her but this time I was going to stay for awhile. I hoped she didn't mind me showin up at her door. I rolled my new Escalade out the garage. I breathed in the cherry air fresher and pressed the play button on the leather steering wheel. "*Your all I need to get by---------------------- Your all I need to get by--------------------Shorty I'm there for u anytime you need me,*" Mary J Bilge and Method Man spit that classic hip hop into the Bose surround sound. I swung my head to the beat accenting its infectious rhythm. I continued to drive down Broad Street and turned right on the Interstate 76. BROOKLYN! Here I come.

The traffic coming into the city was congested for miles as I slowly drove on Interstate 95. I was impatient and losing my temper on the slow moving turnpike. It wasn't until I saw the sign notifying me that I was nearing the Holland Tunnel that I was to feel some relief. After I drove past all the barriers and finally I was crossing the Brooklyn Bridge. I wasn't scared to be driving in Brooklyn it was almost a second home to me. I'd been here shopping all the time and I always wanted to see what it was like living in the largest city in the world. I drove past Juniors and I heard so much about it cheese cake that I wanted to pull over. I continued down Flatbush Ave until I ran into Public Storage facility. I rented the small storage space on the 3rd floor. There I would store the suitcase full of money and the five kilo of dope. Then I decided to put my entire luggage in the storage

HEADGAME   by Brandy

closet and start a new. My decision to start a new meant that I needed a new wardrobe. I locked the closet ensuring it was secured. I strolled to the elevator when I decided to go back to the unit- I forgot to do something. I un-did the locks and didn't bother to turn on the light. I removed the nine millimeter from my purse and placed it in suitcase. I removed the 32 automatic and started to place it in the same place but I stopped. I tucked it back in my bag keeping it for my personal safety. Shit, I be damned if I won't be strapped in New York. I finally reached my cousin on the phone and I was lucky she was home. She was excited to hear from me and insisted that I get there as fast as I could. Her happy voice was just what I needed to cheer me up.

HEADGAME *by Brandy*

Welcome to Brooklyn

Jessie welcomed me to her three stories Brownstone with open arms. Jessie was a bronze skinned beauty with long flowing black hair. She was five foot six inches tall, circular face and she reminded of Janet Jackson. She hugged me so tightly that the air rushed from my lungs.

"Cuzzzo Sup wit ya," I responded as I squeezed her back.

HEADGAME by Brandy

"Oooh You're beautiful," She responded as she looked me up and down. I was wearing my designer Gucci bag, boots and belt to match. Her eyes sparkled when she noticed the ethnicity of my clothes and accessories. Jessie was no slouch and kept up with her clothes and shoe game. Her snake skin boots and Prada bag was hot. We loved clothes and always believed in keeping our shit tight. Jessie worked for the New York Cobra's football team. Her salary was in the mid 40's range. She did the clerical work in the merchandising offices located in the Coliseum. The Coliseum was located in the heart of New York City. Jessie was a straight up gold digger that only dated athletes with seven figure deals. Her last fling was with a married quarterback who brought her a Mercedes Benz c- class. She liked her athletes married so she could play two or three of them at a time.

"So cuzz what bringya up here, Where dat baller at?" She asked as her light brown contacts glistened in the light.

"Ooh Donnie, he's locked up and he'll be away a long time. I wanna start a new so - I'm here," I replied as I didn't get in detail about what was really goin on. I told her about witnessing the death of Carmen and how I wanted to put that behind me. We talked for several hours about the stupid shit we did as kids. I really enjoyed seeing her and having someone to confide in.

"I noticed that you didn't have any luggage," She said.

HEADGAME by Brandy

"I going shopping for an entire new wardrobe tomorrow," I replied as I pulled my hair back looking in the mirror. I was considering changing my hair color and even cutting into a new style.

"Damn bitch you came to buy up Macy's, Look out New York ur new Diva has arrived" She replied making fun of me as I stood in the mirror. I laughed aloud and rolled my eyes. I hadn't laughed in weeks and it was good to let go a little bit. She showed me to the top floor of the Brownstone that was fully furnished apartment. It had a small living room, kitchenette, private bathroom and a large master bedroom with a massive closet. The apartment was so beautiful that it almost made me cry.

"How much do you want for rent?" I asked.

"Girl, did I ask you for money. You can stay here as long as like you. I had a tenant but that nasty bitch had to go," She replied

"No! Do tell," I answered as I braced myself for her story.

"Girl let me tell you, first that bitch had food and dirty clothes stankin up the entire house. I could smell her as soon as I hit the door"

"No get out"

"That's what I told that ass, she had to go... I packed her shit and left it on the door step"

HEADGAME   by Brandy
"You know you ain't right"

"Fuck her.. I work to hard for somebody to be comin in here messin up my shit. Ohh, look at the time we gotta go," She yelled as she shook her hands.

She ran to her room and started putting on the clothes she had laying across the bed. She dressed in a mini skirt and a tight pleaded shirt. She stuffed her thick legs inside riding boots that added to more inches in height. She sprayed the oil sheen over her fully curled hair. She clean her skin with Noxzema wipes and added a light moisturizer to make it shiny. We continued to talk about her tenant and telling jokes. A knock came from the door and it was the chauffeur waiting beside a shiny black Crown Royal that was sent to pick her up. She gathered her purse, cell phone, and keys in one movement. I wasn't prepared to go out socializing. I was looking forward to layin down in my new bed but knowing Jessie she was invited to some big time sports party. I wasn't too fond of athletes and didn't think to much about hanging out with them. I didn't feel comfortable being around them I was used to living with gangtas, thugs and hustla's.

"Aight girl let's go!"

"Go where! I'm not goin anywhere. Look at the way I'm dressed," I replied

"Girl bring your big fat ass on," She said as she grabbed me by the hand and dragged me out the

HEADGAME   by Brandy

door. I tried to make excuses and give reason why I didn't want to go. She wouldn't take no for an answer and I was forced to go with her. Once Jessie made up her mind to do something it was impossible for her to change it. I watched her closely as she touched up her make up and glossed her lips to appear as if she was finished sucking a fat dick. I followed her lead and dolled myself up. In the middle of my prepping it dawned on me that I still didn't know where I was goin. I got nervous and wondered if I would be recognized by anyone from Philadelphia.

"Girl you gonna tell me where we going or what," I asked. "

Ok! OK! The team is having mixer for one of their newest players. Shit girl he just got sign to a nine figure deal and he's fine as hell" a serious look came to her face as she was admitting that she was tryin to catch her athlete.

"Oh he must be married?" I assumed he was because that was her method of operation. She liked her man married and we both knew that.

"No! He ain't married and I'm ready to become a ball player's wife," she said with the most serious look in her eyes.

"Oh what happen to the quarterback," I asked as she cut me off in the middle of my sentence.

"He somewhere makin up with his wife," She replied.

HEADGAME by Brandy

Jessie is my closet cousin but she's ain't nothin but a little freak that's fuckin outta both draws legs. She tryin to settlin down is a load of bull shit. Her ass couldn't settle down if she wanted. I never had known her to stayed true to one nigga in her life. I paid that married shit she was talkin no mind. She liked playing the feild and carrying on in a promiscuous way. I loved her very dearly but it's in her blood.

The car made its way down to Eastern Parkway and over to the Manhattan Bridge. I never liked driving over bridges because they made uncomfortable and I was scared of heights. I wasn't used to being up that high so I tightly closed my eye until we drove into Chinatown. It was a few blocks that we arrived in the village an uppity section of Manhattan. The car rode down 2nd ave until he parked in front of the red carpet outside of Club Ecstasy. The car was idle for moment and it gave me a chance to do some last minute prepping. I took in a deep breath as he opened the door. A small crowd gathered outside waiting for a glance of their favorite football players. I was completely excited as the photographers cameras where flashing and loud music escaping passed it doors. The door was guarded by three hug bouncers that looked as if they were waiting to kick a nigga's ass. When Jessie and I appeared before them we were met with a smile.

"Hey Jess! Sup! whoya friend?" One of the bulky bouncers asked as the others looked on.

HEADGAME   *by Brandy*

"She's with me boys and ya'll should be workin,'" Jess snapped but in a playful manner. I didn't say anything and let Jess handle it all. The two large glass doors where held open by the bouncers as we entered the club. The hostess led us straight to a table next to the VIP. Some scanty ass bitches kept looking at us as if they wanted to get something started. I been around hatin ass bitches before and they had no idea who I was. These bitches where hunting for a football player. Every swinging dick that passed them, they were sizing it up. The fierceness in their eyes and competitiveness was so obvious as they sat around the dance room. Those bitches in the club were half naked and ready to pounce on any player they assumed unwed, free, single and with money. I was there just chillin takin in the party atmosphere and enjoyed listening to the music. I ignored those scheming ass bitches looking for a meal ticket. I wasn't gonna be played by some wanna be, so I ignored them. I hadn't been out clubbing in a long time and it took a minute to get my swagger back. I ordered 5 bottles of Crystal, 4 bottles of Moet and so much food that we weren't able to eat it all. I loved watching the waiter run back and fourth from our table. He ran over people's feet while pushing a small cart filled with food and drink. I would take two or three bites and passed on it. I sipped on my drink as some of Jessie's coworker came over to our table. Mya and Gale came to sit with us or rather *steal our shine* as I wanted to think. They poured drinks, ate with us and started questioning me. They assumed that I was from Hollywood and begun to ask question about celebrities. I played their game and

HEADGAME by Brandy

pretended to have personal ties with Denzel Washington and Jamie Fox. I pretended that I was scouting for locations for my next movie. They continued asking questions about famous people and I sarcastically made up stories about Hollywood gossip. I soon became tired of my charade and their constant questioning.

"What fuck is this twenty question?" I asked. I swung my hair around in a most Diva way. They were convinced that I was from Hollywood and I had studio of connections. After my story telling I retreated to the dance floor because it was only place I could find some peace. All kinds of fake ass players tried to get my attention but I could spot the real nigga from a bootleg wearin fool. Donnie wore the finest suits and didn't mind spending his money on his attire. He liked the new Shawn Carter addition watches, Steve Harvey suits and custom made gator shoes. He wore the best cologne money could buy but preferred Versace or Aramis fragrance. Donnie was a hard act to follow and would be considered a prime catch for any female. While I was with him a lot of people followed him and jockeyed for his attention. He was a mans , man and I missed him at times like these. I loved to watch him work a room as he greeted people nicely with hand shakes and a small kiss on the cheek. His cronies would receive the official pound by knocking fist and bumping shoulders. However since I left my ex I wasn't looking for a real emotional attachments but I was on the prowl for a good piece of dick. I wasn't sure on how was I going to accomplish that but I was horny as shit.

HEADGAME　　　　　　　　by Brandy

I danced several songs while the music enchanted me. I twisted, turned and ignored the howls that were coming from the sidelines. The men attempted to grasp my arm trying to gain my attention while I was on the dance floor. I shrugged my shoulders and ignored them all. I was groovin and settled into my best two step that could I muster. An unfamiliar face came smiling toward me but I didn't care to be bothered. I ignored the attempts for my attention and put more emphasis into my dancing. I turned away with ease and rolled my eyes back. I assumed the person would eventually give up since I was avoiding his advances.

"Ah Vickey," he whispered in my ear.

When I looked hard it was the guy from the airport and I was shocked to see him. He was confident with his approach and it was nice to see such a handsome face. We danced two more songs and I went to sit at my table. When I arrived there an entire crowd had gathered around us. I watched Jessie as she sat in the middle seat talking loudly, waving her glass around and attracting attention. She introduced me to the players that surrounded her. Mya and Gale sat in silence as they soon notice that I had company with me.

"Oh I see you met our host Mike Cardell 1st round draft pick out of Penn State," Jessie said as she shifted her eyes. I smiled ignoring her response. I didn't know that Mike was the guy that she was out for but I didn't care. All they talked about is his number one draft pick but that was gibberish to

HEADGAME by Brandy

me. He must be something special to make all this fuss over. His eyes glistened brighter than the diamond chain draped around his neck and wrist. The bling he sported was truly official as Mike pulled up his chair. He retired to the seat that was next to me and he stayed there for the rest of the night.

"So Miss Vickey I see ur doin a lot better since the last time we met.," he said as he smiled showing me his pearly white teeth. I sized up his chiseled body and wondered how I missed all this sexiness. I glanced at the bulge standing out as if it was greeting me. My pussy started purring and got wet as I wondered about letting him fuck me. It dawned on me that it was along time since a bitch got her shit off. I couldn't take another moment of this slow torture I was putting myself through. I needed to go the bathroom and wipe my pussy off. I was so turned that it was dripping wet. While in the stall Mya came in and confronted me.

"Bitch who brought you here to steal my man?" She said. I could tell that she was drunk by her slurred speech.

" You trippin I know you ain't come in here about some nigga," I responded as I stared her in the eyes coldly.

"I think you ain't heard me right bitch," She replied

"I'm not gonna be to many of your bitches," I warned her as she pointed her finger in my face - which set me off. I punched her in the jaw several

HEADGAME					by Brandy

times which caused the buckling of her legs. She fell to her knees and I grabbed a handful of weave. I then slammed her face into the metal stall. She started to scream and dug her fingernails into my wrist.

"Oh you wanna scratch a nigga!" I yelled as I dragged her narrow ass over the toilet seat and plunged her face into the bowl of piss. She tried fighting me but it was useless as I continue to push her head inside pissy toilet bowl. I tried to drown this stinkin ass heifer. I finally finished using her face as a plunger and left her gasping for air while lying on the floor. I stood over the sink, washed my hands and walked back to my table. I was finish clubbing because that bitch spoiled my mood. I told Jessie what happened and she was ready to kick her ass again. But when I looked up the bouncers where carrying her dumbass toward the back door. I called for my check and Mike offered to pay it. He was caught off guard when he saw my five thousand dollar tab.

"Damn Five grand!" he said as he looked through the receipt.

"I got it! I got it! " I said as I counted off fifty $100 dollar bills and throw it on the table. I stuffed another two hundred dollars in the waiter's hand.

"Imma driveya home," Mike said as he started looking for his keys. I stormed out the party and stopped the first cab I came across. When I turned around I could Mike standing outside the club looking for me. I wanted to reach out to him but I

HEADGAME   *by Brandy*
was ready to go to Brooklyn.

Brand new flava inya ear

After, kicking that bitch's ass in the club I expected no more problems out of her. I was proud at they way I kicked that bitches ass, it had been a long time since I fought with another chick. My last fight with Andrew didn't go well and it had me doubting my skills. I suffered injuries to my hands and needed to care for my wounds. My knuckles were bruised and my hands receive scratches from her nails. I intended on makin a statement by bustin that bitches ass. I was puttin them bitches on

HEADGAME   by Brandy

notice and letting them hoes know that I ain't to be fucked with. Let her step to me again and I won't hesitate goin upside her fuckin head. Jessie laughed until she gagged for air as I told her how I rammed that bitches head in the toilet. I told her how she came into the bathroom stickin her finger my face and confrontin me about some nigga. I demonstrated on how I mopped that bitch over the floor. I could tell she was enjoying the story as she laughed out loudly. Even though Jessie and Maya worked together Jessie had a dislike for her and for professional reasons she was not able to kick her ass. Her only regret was that she was not there to witness Mya's quick demise. Jessie was hysterical as we talked about the details of me kicking Mya's ass.

"I don't know what that bitch had in her mind but I bet she regrets ever fuckin witya," Jessie laughed

"Ya know that bitch is gonna feel that ass whippin in the mornin, Cause I was not playin wit that bitch"

"I wish I was there cause I can't stand that hatin ass bitch, I'm so glad you shut her fuckin mouth for once and for all"

"Cuz ya shoulda seen it , I had the bitch screamin for help as I had stuffed that bitches face in that pissy ass toilet water"

"Ahhh Mann. Don't say any more ur killin me"

"She really made me mad when she splashed that piss on my Gucci Shoes. If they're permanently

HEADGAME   *by Brandy*

stained, the next time I see her - Imma kick that bitches ass again"

"You need to stop it girl"

Jessie knew that I had no problems with kickin a bitch's ass. While growing up she witnessed me in action and I dared anyone to try me. I soak my hands in ice and waited for some of the swelling to subside. I was exhausted from all the excitement and the lack of sleep. Jessie crawled up the steps to her room to attend to her company. She managed to pick up some guy and as usual her hot ass was going to fuck him. I'm not one to judge but I didn't see why she went on like that. It wasn't like she was starving and was doing it for money. She was a little loose and looking for love in all the wrong places. I stayed in the living room and remembered the highlights of my night and seeing that scrumptious ass nigga Mike. I was exhausted from the fighting, traveling and an arguing. I swallowed a handful of pains pills and waited for the effects to come over me. It was after a few drinks that I was at the point of exhaustion this is when I'm able to find any kind of sleep. It was only for a couple of hours at a time that I succeeded in finding some rest.

Not being able to sleep has been effecting Since I murdered the twins. Dealing with my anger, vengeance and conscious I developed insomnia. I laid awake must nights with my memories circling in my head. I didn't rest for very long. I was awake three hours later soberly looking at the four walls. It was then I look through my photo album searching

HEADGAME   by Brandy

for reminders of my past life. I added some pictures since the last time I looked through it. I stared at the picture with my parents holding me and smiling. The pictures took me to my happy place and it was only then I could have good thoughts. I thumbed through the album and the pictures of Carmen changed my mood. I closed the album and hid it from myself. It was almost 4am and I was hearing animalistic noises coming from Jessie room. I was hearing Jessie moaning explicitly as the bed post knocked against the wall. I enviously turned on the radio to drown out her howling.

The next morning I walked in Jessie's room to wake her and unsurprisingly she was not alone. My curiosity got the better of me and I couldn't help to see who it is so I peeked to see who was sleeping in her room. I wondered if the person she bought in was Mike and if so I was ready to cut his throat. Luckily it was somebody else I hadn't seen him before and a murder was avoided. I shrugged my shoulders and guessed she let a nigga fell asleep in her pussy. I walked back upstairs leaving Jessie and her companion to continue snoring. I showered and changed my clothes readying myself for the day. I picked up my purse to see if I still had everything in my bag especially my gun. I removed the bullets from the clip and pulled back barrel of the gun. It automatically throw a bullet out of the chamber and landed on the bed. I was considering disarming myself by leaving my gun in the drawer. The warning I received from JJ and the $100, 000 still lingering over my head made me think twice. I reloaded the weapon as I placed it

HEADGAME   by Brandy

back in my bag until I was sure that I was safe. I was dressed and ready to go shopping and I remembered that I promised Jessie that I was going to take her with me. Jessie had good taste in clothes and her experience would be needed. I called Jessie on her cell phone and it rang several times before she answered.

"Girl ya need to get up"

"Why Saturday? I gotta hangover and I'm tired"

"Im going shoppin, so if ya wanna go, you need to geta move on"

"Shopping Trip!," She yelled into the phone.

That bitch was dressed and ready to go in twenty minutes flat. She damned near put the nigga out butt naked because he wasn't movin fast enough. She knew how I rolled when it was time to go shoppin and how I spent money. I was ready to buy me some cloth's. I loved the high I got from shopping and how gaves me a needed boost. The bags, new clothes and the ringing of the credit card machine got me excited. I hadn't been shopping since finding my new found wealth. My hands where itching to spend some of that money. A queen needs the right attire to rule her subjects.

It was day to remember as we raided the shops along Fifth Avenue. Gucci, Prada, Louie, Juicy Couture, Channel and Jewelry from Tiffany & Co. I walked the entire Macys buying Baby Phat, Kenneth Cole and JLo. It took me approximately 8

HEADGAME by Brandy

hours and to spend sixty thousand dollars. We hired a black car and chauffeur to carry all the bags to our house. All the shopping gave me an appetite and decided that we stop at Juniors for something to eat. Jessie drove us to Brooklyn and the chauffeured limo follow with our packages. We parked on Atlantic avenue in the crowded streets of Brooklyn. We walked to the restaurant and we soon found ourselves sitting in the booth waiting for servers to take our orders. Since the drive back to Brooklyn I could tell that something was eating her. I couldn't take it her as she rolled her eyes and gasped loudly. She finally got up enough heart to say what's on her mind.

"Girl tell me again how you got all this money. I mean you tossed five grand at the club and sixty grand in those stores. I ain't tryin to be newsy but can I get in on it," She asked as she waited for tho response. I really wanted to tell her the truth but I knew it would've been to complicated for me so I lied.

"Donnie left me a nice piece change and wanted to make sure I was bein looked after when he got locked up. I'm spending his dope money." I answered as I searched her face for a reaction.

"How much did he leave you if don't mind me askin," She inquired.

"Damn that's a real private question,"

"I'm sorry Vickey for bein curious. You don't think you can trust me?

HEADGAME by Brandy

"It's just a long story and one day I'll tellya"

"Aight.. I get it"

"Did you like those Prada Shoes?"

I changed the conversation as we sat at the table. She got the message that I wasn't gonna tell her anything else. She know better to keep asking but from now on I was more aware of what I said and how much money I would reveal. We gobbled up the hamburger and fries sent by the cook. Within an hour we arrived at the Brownstone and a large box was sitting on front door.

Jessie walk toward the box and picked it up. I leaned behind the car expecting a explosion. She leaned down and pulled the cover off the box. I watched her eyes open wide with surprise.

"Wait! Wait" I folded my arms covering my head expecting see a flash of fire from an explosion.

"Look its roses and a card, It must be for me" She slowly picked up unfolded the card to read it

"What's it say?"

"My bag its for you, its from Mike" as she handed the box to me

"oh for me" I was surprised by such a sweet gesture and horrified by the thoughts that it was a bomb. I was standing in shocked as my heart pounded through my shirt. I was sure it was a

HEADGAME   by Brandy

bomb and it was going to explode. I thought we where going to die any moment as II waited for the fire and shrapnel. I hoped she didn't recognize the stressful look on my face and how strangely I acted. I hid my nervous reaction by gathering my composure quickly. I snatched the note outta her hand and I was excited to read it myself. I uncrumbled the card and read the content on the paper.

roses are red

violets are blue

You ain't have to run off

does it mean we're through

I smiled when received his card and I wondered if I was ready to have a new relationship. I was still bitter on how things went down with Donnie and I needed sometime by myself. I wasn't sure how long I was gonna stay in Brooklyn but it was okay for now. I tried to stay to myself but Jessie took the liberty of giving Mike my phone number and he made every attempt to get my attention. It wasn't until the first game of the season that I would see Mike again. If it wasn't for the box seats I would've stayed home but the promise of a goodtime and drama free was too tempting. I wore my team jersey with Mike's number on it with my tightest jeans and baseball cap. I arrived at the stadium only to find that I was in company of the famous rapper Terror Tee and his entourage. They were loud and filled the sky box with weed smoke. The

HEADGAME   by Brandy

large windows gave you a view of the entire field and you could hear all the talk on the sideline over the intercom. It was an outstanding view of the game that took my breath away. Even though I have no idea of what was goin on and I didn't know the difference between a touchdown or a homerun. I cheered when everybody else did and I held my breath every time Mike ran with the ball. As I watched the game I caught the eye of Terror Tee with his platinum teeth and chain to match. I particularly didn't like his music and his shit was straight out whack. His latest album "knockin em off" was certified gold in two days its first release "ohh ahh whatup with ya," was number on the charts. It was the stupidest song that I ever heard. His southern drawl made the words to the song undetectable and beat was like a Master P rip-off. I hoped to god he would leave me alone but unfortunately at half time Terror Tee made his way over to me.

"Heynow der shawty," He said as he step to my face. I got wind of his breath and it smelled like shit. I don't know if a little man walked into his mouth and took a shit on his tongue. It was humming like a mother fucker and I couldn't bear him talking to me. I didn't know if it was the weed, the platinum teeth, liquor or cigarettes but his breath was stankin. I moved away and covered my face.

"Wow!" I yelled. He was not used to people moving away so abruptly but I couldnt take the horrible smell that wreaked from his mouth- not today. His crew witnessed my embarressing reaction toward

HEADGAME   by Brandy

him and began to instigate by making sound effects with their mouths. It made situation seem more than it was.

"Oooooooo," the crew yelled out which caused Terror to get embarrassed.

"Ah Bitch you tryna dis me... Fuk u den bitch! Fuk u den bitch!" he yelled out trying to save face.

"I ain't a bitch. yoo momma's a bitch," I replied as I got out the seat and covered my entire face tryin to hide from the stank of his breathe.

"Dat bitch dono who I iz," He said as he turned toward the entourage.

"Yea me and toothpaste don't know you nigga. Damn! Damn!" I shouted as I hold up my hands signaling I didn't want to talk with him.

"Fukyu den shawty, Fuckyu den shawty," He said as he waved his hand away from me. He turned to his crew and walked toward them. They where in shock and speechless as if they never witnessed Terror Tee get dissed so badly before.

"lite up dat deer smoke , she ain't nuffin" He said as he stood over his crew. Since the confrontation they left me alone and tried to make remarks about me. I paid that shit no mind and I really ain't feeling like kickin some bitch's ass over the bullshit. So I pretended like I didn't hear their snob jokes they were telling. Jesse came to the booth and took me to the field with all the players. I was amazed at the

HEADGAME   by Brandy

loud cheering and the excitement that filled the stadium. I caught they eye of the star running back as he winked at me. I waved at him and smiled. I was truly happy to see him and for the first time I admitted to myself that I may have a small crush on Mike.

After the game all the players crowded into club Ecstasy to celebrate their victory over the opposite team. I was sitting at the bar waiting for Mike to arrive. I was tired of playing hard to get and I would allow Mike some time if it wasn't too late. I was tired of finger fucking myself; it was time to get me a piece of dick. I contemplated our conversation when I was interrupted by a now drunken Terror Tee.

"AHHH Y'ALL, looka here we got us dis uppity bitch, bartender giz dis bitch a drink on me, " He said as he grabbed my arm and twisted me around. I picked up my glass and throw my drinks in his face. The red wine soiled his solid white shirt and pants as it dripped down. He swelled up his chest and grabbed me by the arm.

"Get the fuck off me!" I yelled at him. He raised his hand and ready himself to swing. I thought to reach for my bag but it was too late and all I could do was brace myself for the impact. I closed my eyes and held up my hands attempting to protect myself.

"Bitch!" Terror Tee yelled and pulled his hand back as if to slap me. He was stopped before he could get his hand to my face. Mike tackled him to the floor and smashed two table as they hit the floor.

HEADGAME   by Brandy

Mike placed his large hands around his neck and begun to choke the life out the boy. His crew was attempting to step in but was met by half of Mike's football team. The bouncers broke up the fight and escorted Terror Tee and his crew out the door. Mike dusted himself off and spoke to me about the matter at hand.

"Damn girl ya always in some shit. What was his problem" Mike said as he grabbed me by the waist.

"I don't know what his problem comin in here grabbin up on me," I responded

He picked up my bag and quickly noticed the gun sitting on top.

"Damn! Whatya gonna do wit that?" He asked with surprise in his voice. I snatched my bag and walk past him avoiding his questions.

"What you a Cop know?," I responded by pulling away from him as he attempted to talk with him.

"OK, OK You don't have to say it like that but come sit with me. I've been tryna to holla at you for awhile and you keep avoidin me, "He said as he grabbed my arm softly and whispered in my ear.

"Im not a avoiding you probably get all the attention you need with all the groupies around," I said as I shifted my eyes around.

HEADGAME by Brandy

"Its all part of the being a ball player but I wanna get to know you Vickey, not them." He said brushing my hand.

"Oh I know your kind all smooth and charming until you get what you want," I said being slick at the tongue.

"First of all I can get all the sex I want but I'm lookin for someone special and I see that in you," He said looking into my eyes. I explained that I was coming out of a bad relation and in the middle of a healing process. I told him that my ex boyfriend was a very dangerous and I carried the gun for my protection.

"Vickey all you need is for somebody to take care of you and I'm gonna be that guy, "He said. We talked for hours when he realized that he needed to go the airport for an out of town football game. He asked me if I didn't mind accompanying him to the airport. This was a perfect plan to spend some quality time together. We walked to the car when two men attacked us. Mike was knocked to the floor and they kicked him viciously to the ribs.

"Get off him," I said as I pushed the assailant away from Mike. "Slap!" He hit me so hard I slammed against the car and fell into the gutter. I rose to my feet and reached for my gun hidden in my purse.

Blocka! Blocka! Blocka! I fired three warning shots in the air. The man jumped back and yelled like a little bitch.

HEADGAME   by Brandy

"That bitch gotta gun!," they said as they started ran away. I aimed the gun at them, targeting the assailant's chest. I was locked on one of them and ready to pull the trigger.

"Haaa Whatya doin," Mike said as he grabbed my arm before I could get off my shot. Luck was on their side because if it wasn't for Mike somebody would be dead in the parking lot. We sat in his limo, took a ride to JFK airport and talked about our run in with Terror Tee's goons.

"You was really gonna shot em!"

"Ah yeah, he was tryin to hurt you"

"Damn Vickey I ain't never seen a female like you. You don't take no shit, you pay your own way and your loyal. I need someone like you to watch a my back"

"Loyal! Oh you can tell all that. "

"Yes I can"

"Whoever hurtya I'm sorry but Ill never do you like that"

"I heard that before"

"I betya have"

The limo arrived at the airport and after a brief hug; I was turned around from my trip home. While driving to Brooklyn I looked out the window and

HEADGAME   *by Brandy*

was considering staying in New York a little longer. I was having fun and enjoying my new found company.

A Brush with Death

HEADGAME   by Brandy

I sent Mike off hours ago and already I could not wait until he returned back from his trip. Even tough we didn't fuck like I wanted too. I still wanted to be next to him and enjoyed his company. It was so long ago that I had the feeling of wanting someone. I was excited but it felt so unusual for me to be acting in such a giddy way. I was already grinning like a big ass kool aid smile when ever I spoke his name. He promised that as soon as he settled in a hotel that he would call me. I hoped he was thinking of me as I was him. I wanted to believe that I found someone that was sincere and considerate to me. I could always tell when a dude was lying to me. I found Mike to be truthful and honest. Mike finally called me and I was so excited to get his call.

" I've been thinkin of you since you left"

"Havya, what you been thinking about?"

"Where's a girl like you come from?

"Philly.. West Philly to be exact"

"oh ok, where 's ya family at? "

"My Dad got killed and my Mom is in a home for her problems"

"I'm sorry to hear that"

While we where talking on the phone I explained to him that I was raised from the gutters of West Philly. I explained how my mother had lost her

HEADGAME by Brandy

mind doing drugs and how my father was killed. I even talked of my ex and how I escaped him. I avoided telling Mike how I'm set him up for his fall but he didn't need to know about that.

"Vickey when I looked into your eyes I could see the pain and the hurt. I can tell you are a really good person who doesn't trust easily but I want you to trust me because I will never hurt you." He said.

I believed that he would never hurt me like Donnie and I really wanted give him a chance. I decided to keep myself open and forget the past. I was feeling confident about how things were goin for us. We talked so long we didn't realize it was getting late. He needed to rest for the big game he was playing in tomorrow. We said our good byes and finally hung up the phone.

As soon as the phone hit the receiver Jessie was anxiously waiting details of my progress. She was attempting pry into my business as she asked about my phone call. It made me uncomfortable and I was reluctant to give details but Jessie was cool. So I entrusted her with the business and gave up the 411.

"So girl whenya hit dat,"She asked. I immediately twisted my lips and rolled my eyes.

"Don't tell me you ain't git none yet- get outta here. If that was me Id take dat nigga like this and give em some this." She said as she popped her ass like a gogo dancer.

HEADGAME   by Brandy

"Oh shut up.. He's on that gentleman shit and he wants us to take our time,"

"He betta hurry and giveya ass some dick cause a bitch like you might kill somebody," she said with a loud laugh.

"I don't see nothin funny about a bitch being thirsty for some dick," I said

"Do you like him?"

"He's aight.. I mean he's kool"

"Don't stunt on me girl"

"Alright I like him"

"I'm happy for you because you deserve to be happy"

I walked up the stairs to my room for some much needed rest. I heard my phone ringing agian and I knew that it was Mike calling me back. The caller Id displayed Margi and that gave me such a big surprise. I hesitated answering her call at first but I was eager to hear from my old friend and what she had to say. Since I hadn't heard from her in a couple of months, I thought it was strange to receive a call for her at such a late hour.

"Hello!," I answered.

"Vickey is that you?

HEADGAME   by Brandy
"Hey girl howya been?" I answered

"Where are you? Is your mother still at that nursing? Are you comin back to Philly soon? she asked.

"I know you ain't call me asking me all these questions, what doya want from me?" I screamed into the phone.

"You ain't gotta get like that Vickey I'm the one who helped you clean up that shit remember," She retorted.

"I know what you did for me but that don't mean you can call me any time you like and interrogate me," I said. She upset me by the way that she talked to me so grimy and disrespectful. The way she mentioned our past dealings I was worried that she was recording our conversation.

"I called because I'm having problems with changing the name on the property and I need us to go to the clerk office. The property is still in your name and you need to sign it over to me there to make it official. " she said

" I don't think I can make it to Philly because I have so much to do out here." I said regretfully.

"You promised me the building and I want what's comin to me," She added with a change of tune.

"So what you tryna say Margi?" I asked.

HEADGAME by Brandy

"Maybe the police need to hear about a certain murder I knew about," She added

"Huh whatya say to me?" I asked.

I wished she was right there so I could of snatched the weave right outta her head. How dare she even try to come at my neck like that?

"You need to have your ass down here in two days or Im goin to the police. Did you get that? I'm tired of mutha fuckas like you who think they can just use people and throw them away."She screamed into the phone.

"First of all I giveya seventy five thousand and a building for you troubles-BITCH!," I yelled into the phone.

"You only gave me pennies, bitch and I don't feel rightly compensated from my time and work"

"Just tell me what you want"

"Your ass betta be here in 48 hours or I'mma tell the police about a bad little girl who likes to rob and kill "

"Ill be there in two of days, Ill call you when I'm on the way," I conceded.

"AHHH thats wonderful I can't wait to see you its been so long. I'm gonna need another seventy five thousand dollars"

HEADGAME by Brandy

"Another seventy five grand.. You greedy ass bitch I ain't got that type of money"

"You lyin ass bitch, word is you got a lot more than your tellin, I want my 10 percent of that 1.5 million you got that's one hundred fifty thousand. since ya already give me seventy five you owe me another"

"Don't the building count for anything"

"Yeah it does that's why its only seventy five grand"

"aight but this is the last time Im gonna pay you. If you ever try blackmail me again then Im gonna killya? .

"Donnie's pretty concerned with you and he asked me to give you a message," She responded.

"A MESSAGE!"

"He says he ain't mad at you for what you did and he still loves you"

"Is that it?"

"Yeah that's it and get here with my money"

"How do I know you ain't settin me up?"

"I guess you'll have to trust me. Bye Vickey I'll seeya later"

I hung up the phone and lay across the bed. I knew her slimy ass setting to set me up. I weighed out

HEADGAME by Brandy

my options and thought hard before I made a decision to go back to Philadelphia. I didn't want to go by myself so I decided that I would take Jessie with me. She was a new face and no one would suspect her of spying for me. I needed her to agree to go with me but I wouldn't use lying or trickery to get her to ride with me. I would tell her the truth and let her know the high stakes I was playing for. I went down stairs and ordered the take out Chinese food. We ate it in the diving room. I wanted to tell her the real problems so I decided to be straight up and asked her to come with me.

"Jessie, I gotta go to back to Philadelphia to handle some business. Can you to come with me?" I asked.

"Sure Vickey I can go with. I just take a few days off from work." she answered.

"Before you agree ...I haven't been honest with you all the way...What i need to tell you is that I ripped off my boyfriend and put his sorry ass in jail because he cheated on me, I had to kill his second in command because he tried to rape me, the girl I want you to check on is the only one that can prove that I committed murder. She's threatening to turn states evidence on me. I rewarded her loyalty by giving her money and property but she's attempting to black mail me for seventy five thousand dollars more. I need you to watch over me while I'm seeing what that slimy bitch is really up to. I don't trust her and want you to have my back. I got a feelin that she's settin me up and I'm gonna need an ace in the hole. I ll giveya fifty thousand for going and if anything ever happens Ill

HEADGAME   by Brandy

show where my stash is. I managed to recoup a little more money than I told you about. It's a little over a million dollars and it's yours I don't make back." I said. I was hopeful that the lure of money would encourage her to accept.

"Fiddy G's I'm in," She replied.

"I needya to be ready in 30 minutes."

"I gotta work tomorrow but Imma call in sick and then we can ride out"

"Are you sure that you wanna go? This could be dangerous?

"I'm cuz I got your back no matter what"

I was so excited that Jessie decided to take this trip to Philadelphia with me. Jessie is a thorough ass female and that would fight until the very end. Growing up we'd teamed up and kicked some bullies asses. She wouldn't run if the going got tough or threatened. Her nerves were steady and she had a killer's streak just like her father. Even though I was nervous and worried Jessie reassured me that everything was gonna be alright. This was unusual for us not be laughing and joking around. Thinking of what I was going to face I remained silent as I packed and prepared for the trip to Philadelphia. We sat our carry on bags inside my car and drove toward the location of the storage unit. When we where driving toward our destination I reached in my bag, revealing to her my hidden weapon.

HEADGAME by Brandy

"Do you know how to use one of these?" I asked as I waved the 32 automatic in her face.

"You know I was brought up in the Military," She said as she grab the gun like a pro, pulled the clip out and freed the chambered round with one motion. She took apart the gun into three pieces and put it back together quickly. Jessie toyed with the weapon and when she finished returned to me. I suggested that she keep it but she refused my request. She reached in her purse and showed off her chromed plated semi auto forty five caliber. The large hand guns dwarfed her small hands as she showed them off. I tucked my weapon into my purse as I parked beside the reaking dumpster. We exited the vehicles and we made our way into building housing my storage unit. I unlocked and opened the metal door. I stepped inside the dark room and turned on the lights. I grabbed the suitcase and unzipped it revealing the large sums of cash. I showed her the diamonds, fur coats and the five bricks of heroin that I stashed. I searched inside the suit case for the nine-millimeter Smith and Wesson I killed Andrew with. I counted out seventy thousand in cash and give her twenty five grand. I placed the other fifty grand and the guns in my favorite Gucci bag.

"Only thing I'm askin you to do is take care of my mother," I asked. She nodded in agreement and I closed the storage closet. While sitting in the vehicle the silence seemed to stress the moment. I pressed the play button triggering the music to be ripped through the air giving us the sweetest vibes. "Ya all I need to get bye------------------ Mary J

HEADGAME   *by Brandy*

Blige sang out " We moved our heads to the bass line and tapped our hands to the beat of the music. We danced in our seats care free and with no worry of what lay ahead.

HEADGAME   by Brandy

A brush with death

When we arrived in Philly it was close to 10:30 pm. I wanted to rest and to find a nice place to sleep. I decided to drive to the luxurious Marriott between 13th and Market Street. We stayed in the penthouse suite over lookin the city of brotherly love. I encouraged Jessie to get some rest while I took a look around the city. She asked to drive with me but I didn't want her identity to be revealed to anyone. I couldn't afford to run into anybody I knew or be seen with my ace in the hole. I decided to drive to Upper Darby where I killed the twins at. I wanted to see if anybody was living there. I parked down the street with a clear view of the front door The second floor light was on and I wondered who could be staying at the house. I sat outside for an hour and no one seemed to be there. I didn't want to take a chance on getting caught entering the house. I called Domino's pizza and ordered food using the address. It seemed like it took forever for the pizza to come. When the Pizza man knocked on the door I could tell it was a female that answered the door. It was very difficult for me to identify who she was. I picked my brain and thought hard about whom was the lady living in our house. The lady looked liked Chyna but I though she was in jail with Donnie.

HEADGAME by Brandy

I made my way back to the Marriott and by this time Mike was blowing up my phone. I told him that I was going outta town on some very important family business and I would be back in a couple days. He asked me If I was going to see my ex which I denied. So I decided to make up another lie - I told him that my mother was ill and I going to the mental hospital to visit her. He sounded as if he still didn't believe me but I didn't care. When I got back to the room Jessie was watching old reruns of Good Times. I parked my ass in front of the TV and drank in every word the Evans Family said. I loved watchin the old sitcom because it was one of the few times in my life when I could remember my mother acting normal. She loved to laugh at JJ and Thelma fighting over the smallest things. I thanked Jess for being here and helping with this problem called Margi. I didn't trust her and I knew Jess would have my back

The next morning we showered, got dressed and ate a large breakfast. It was 10 am when we drove to the hair salon Margi now owned. She painted the outside green and yellow with her name across the door way "MARGI's". It was the most hideous thing I ever did see. The shop was still closed when we got there. I noticed the for sale sign hanging in the window that me pissed me off. She failed to mention she was trying to sell the building. We sat around waiting for somebody to open up the salon. Margi drove past in a new Lexus ES and draped in a new Sable coat. Her hair was longer than I remember and pulled into a bob. The

HEADGAME   by Brandy

diamonds on her neck and ears were blinged out. The crisp diamonds radiated from her body and blinded anyone looking directly at her. I wasn't used to seeing Jessie all glamorous like that and it was then I realized what she spent the first seventy five thousand dollars on. Jessie exited the car a block away from the salon. I told her to listen out for my call to Margi while sitting in the waiting. Jessie wore her new snug fitting Baby Phat body suit and some white Nikes. She also wore a white baseball cap to cover her head and to hide her appearance. Jessie had an outburst when I suggested that she would have to go get hair done by people she didn't trust. I watched as she opened the door and went inside the salon. I waited in the car so I could prepare myself for Margi's shitty ass attitude. I took a deep breath and I dialed Margi's number. Her annoying caller tune caught me off guard;" How did you got here, nobody supposed to be here" the caller tune was interrupted when she answered.

"Hello," she answered.

" Hi Margi and I will be in town around noon so why don't you meet me at City Hall," I said

"You don't control shit Vickey Imma tellya what you are gonna do. When you arrive you need to have my seventy thousand dollars. Meet me at the McDonald's located on Broad and Girard at 1pm. If you don't show or have my doe then I'm goin straight to the Police," She yelled into the phone. I tried to respond to her demands but before I could answer she hung up the phone. I knew that this

HEADGAME by Brandy

would be trouble for me but I needed to think quickly. I didn't have any choice but to meet her at 1pm. I called Jessie and told her to meet me at the car. She walked up the street and sat in the car awaiting the message. I told her that I would have to meet Margi at the McDonalds on Broad street and Girard Avenue. The meeting place was across town but I could make the drive in 30 minutes. I sat in the car across the street, stuffed the brown paper bag with twenty thousand and adjusted the nine millimeter in my purse. I crossed the street and entered the McDonalds stationed on the corner. The smell of fried food made me hungry and I contemplated ordering some food. I resisted the temptation to order me something to eat and sat close to the window so I could see the cars driving into the parking lot. It was already 1:30pm when she decided to arrive for the meeting. Her Lexus stood out as she drove between the golden arches parking space. She recognized me despite my change of appearance and signaled to me by waving her hand. I was quickly drawn me to the car while noticing she had no passengers with her. I sat in the passenger seat and she pushed a loaded thirty eight snub nose into the side of my ribs.

"Vickey don't move so fast, hands on the dash board. "She said as she forced the gun barrel into my ribs.

"Okay, I thought we was meeting like close friends Margi?" I said as I complied with the order and started to reach up for the dashed board. I spread my arms apart and reached out to touch the

HEADGAME *by Brandy*

dashboard when I was given a blinding blow to the side of my head. SMACK!

"Ooouch!" I yelled as I grabbed my head feeling the sharp pains caused by blow. I soon felt a wet sensation of blood trickling down my head.

"That was for getting me involved in this bullshit," She said as she grabbed my bag and searched my body finding my thirty two semi auto tucked between my legs. I was rewarded with another blow across the head. SLAP!

"Ahhhhh!," I cried out as the force of the blow made stars appear before my eyes. She looked inside my purse and found the money sitting in the bag next to another loaded to the gun. She counted out the money loudly.

"Two guns, what was you plannin to do with them ?

"Nothin?"

"All the fuck you brought me is twenty grand...Bitch what the fuck I'm supposed to with dat," She said as she threatened me with her weapon by pressing it to the side of my head.

"Your gonna meet your maker today bitch"

"Fuck You bitch you ain't gettin another dime more...FUCK YOU!" I yelled defiantly.

That pissed her off as she hit me with the butt of her weapon. I tried to take cover from her attack,

HEADGAME by Brandy

blocking her blows and trying not to allow her hit me with another forceful blow. I tried to fight her and before I could swing my knock out punch I was met with a taser sending 100,000 volts to my body. "ZAAAAP!" I was immediately rendered helpless as I was bound and gagged.

When I regained consciousness I was blind folded with my hands tied behind my back and my feet were tied together. I no longer heard Margi's annoying ass voice as the cold truck floor I was laying on was planted against my face. The Vans super charger V8 engine rumbled as it took me to my unknown destination. I knew that I was going to be painfully tortured or killed. I was so frightened that I begun to cry and beg to my capturers.

"Leeet meee go, Let me go," I cried as the snot and tears joined at the bottom of my cheeks. I vision a most horrible death ready to befall me.

"Shut the fuck up bitch!" The lady shouted as she ripped off my blindfold to reveal her identity

"Chyna?" I yelled as I recognized her face looking at me.

"Yeah bitch it's me and Donnie sends his love. I got some payback for your ass. Donnie didn't appreciate you snitching on us and since he can't be here I gonna kill you. First I'm gonna put a bullet in both your legs and make you wish you were a dead, bitch," She said. She smashed my nose into

HEADGAME   by Brandy

the side of the metal truck panels. Chyna pulled the gun back, chambering a live round and pointed it to my head. I knew I was dead so I started to make my peace with God.

"Our orders from Donnie are not to kill dat bitch until we find the money," The man driving said. Chyna turned around to answer the man but she was interrupted when the large Escalade smashed into the side of the van. The impact of the crash caused the vans rear wheels to leap off the ground. This caused Chyna to shot off three rounds as she fell to the ground. Blocka! The first stray bullet missed my head by three inches. Blocka! The second stray bullet went through roof of the van which let a spot of light shine in. Blocka! The third shot shattered parts of the windshield and showered glass all over the drivers face. The van swerved in and out traffic while crashing against several parked cars. The van excelled as his foot pressed heavily on the gas pedal as he panicked from specs of broken glass digging into his eyes. The driver attempted to press the brake and bring the Van to a halt. The black Escalade violently side swiped the van the caused it to crash into the wooden telephone pool sending everything that wasn't tied down flying. My face collided with the back of passenger seat while Chyna and the driver were thrown out the window of the Van.

To my surprise it was Jessie removing the debris that was covering me and helping me from van. I was thankful she was freeing me from my captivity. I closed my eyes and started to pray because I knew that I escaped death clutches again. I only

HEADGAME by Brandy

wished that the pain in my head would end. I stumbled into the Escalade with my blurry vision and Jessie drove away from the accident. Jessie wanted to take me to the hospital but I refused to go. I needed to pay my good friend Margi a visit. We drove to her salon and waited outside for her to go home. I passed out leaving Jessie alone to watch the salon.

"Get up Getup ," Jessie shouted so she woke me from my sleep.

"What?" I asked.

"I'mma follow her when she pulls off ," she said

I watched her walk to her car and that's when I noticed she'd stolen my brand new Gucci bag. She so kindly had it wrapped around her arm as if she'd pay for it.

"Ooh I want my fuckin bag back," I said as I almost ran out the truck. We drove behind her following her every turn and stop. She led us to a residential neighborhood out in Northeast section of town. She drove into the two car garage and closed the door behind her. We parked outside her new and fancy two story house looking to see if she had company.

"You stay here I need to handle this alone," I said as I grabbed her forty five automatic and walked toward her house. Despite my ego being shattered and suffering some bumps and bruises I was ok. My injured legs caused me to walk with a limp. The

HEADGAME   *by Brandy*

closer I walked to the house the angrier I became for her part in my betrayal. I checked the front door and the back door both were locked. I noticed a slight opening in the kitchen window that I could climb through. Margi moved across room and made her way upstairs. I silently climbed through the open kitchen window. I was angered and excited to see my stolen purse sitting on the dining room table. I slowly and quietly climbed up the steps while taking precautions not to make any alerting sounds. I heard the bath water splashing as it filled the tub. I raised my gun and aimed it toward the closed bathroom door. I kicked the bathroom door in and she was standing over the tub wrapped in a bath robe.

"You stinkin bitch! You stole my fuckin bag," I said as I aimed my gun at her chest.

"Wait, I gotta tellya something you need to know," She said

"Well bitch you ain't got that long so you betta spill it,"

"I didn't want to set you up Vickey but they made me do it. The Africans has a one hundred thousand dollar contract on you, for killin their two brothers in that botched up robbery. Donnie offered me another fifty thousand to locate you. You're a dead woman and it's only a matter of time they was gonna find ya. They threatened to kill me if I didn't help them. They was gonna kill me Vickey, I'm sorry I'm sorry" She said as she fell into a ball and started pleading for her life.

HEADGAME   by Brandy

"I'm not gonna killya but Imma giveya dis ass woopin you got comin to ya first," I said.

I carefully unloaded my gun and placed it on the toilet seat. I balled up my fist and invited her to come get some. The bitch rushed me with so much force that I fell backwards against the wall. We fell over then started wrestling on the floor. She punched me twice while I pulled her weave making a loud ripping noise.

"Ahhh," She yelled as she rolled over and grabbed her scalp feeling for the missing pieces of hair. I stood in the doorway with a large piece of weave waving in front of her face. She charged me again but this time I side step her allowing her to go head first into the wall. I grabbed her by the back of her neck and ripped what was left of her weave. I carelessly slammed her face first into the mirrors sending glass shards all over the floor. I beat her face into the sink knocking loss several front teeth and causing extreme gashes over her face. I bombarded her ribs with several violent kicks that accented my statement.

"Don't you ever in your life touch my purse you stinkin bitch," I said. After I finished kicking the living shit out of her ,I gathered my belonging and collected my stolen Gucci bag. I returned to the car, opened the front door and sat with the now angry Jessie. I could tell by the looks in her eyes that she upset because I didn't finish her off.

"You gonna let that bitch live, Fuck that stupid double crossin hoe," she said as she exited the car

HEADGAME by Brandy

and walked inside the house. I sat in the car and patiently waiting for Jessie to finish the job. Blocka! Blocka! Blocka! Echoed from the house alerting me to sounds of the gun. Jessie exited from the house and walked to the car with no remorse for sending Margi to the grime reaper.

We sped away from scene of the crime I but still felt like I needed to burn down her hair salon. I wanted to destroy her memory and the legacy she was building. Even though I was beaten up and half conscious I wasn't ready to go back to Brooklyn. We drove to the hair salon and Jessie sat quietly as I removed the two bottles from the back. I ignited the rags hanging from two bottles filled with gasoline. I tossed them throw the large front window causing it to spill the incendiary substances into the darkened room. Seconds later the flames spread rapidly though out the first floor. The fire engulfed the building and its flames shattered the windows with its 400 degree heat. I slowly shifted the car into drive and the engine accelerated toward my chosen direction. A proud feelin came over me as I thought of how I was able survive my close brush with death.

HEADGAME by Brandy

A player life for me

It had been three months since my brush with death while I was in Philadelphia. I healed from my stitches to the back of my head and my arm was wrapped in a sling. Mike was upset with me keeping secrets and refused to believe that I went to see my Mom. He avoided me for weeks never saying a word to me. I attempted to call his cell phone but all I got was his voicemail. Jessie came up with the idea that I should ambush him at the club so I can get into his good graces. Jessie was tired of seeing me sad by this situation and decided to intervene of my behalf. Her connections with the team allowed us to have access to the team party with out any problems from security. I wore the tightest little black dress I could find with my come fuck me pumps. I spent hours at the salon getting my hair styled and making sure it was looking just right. When I was finished dressing and looked in the mirror, my looks resembled my mother so much. I had that killers stare in my eyes and the beauty of a princess. I didn't want to make a fool of myself and throw myself at his feet. I wanted us to continue getting close and put the past behind us.

HEADGAME   by Brandy

When I arrived at the club the outside bouncers greeted me with love and respect.

"Ms. Vickey, Damn girl ya sure looking fine tonight"

"Thanks boys, how ya'll doin"

"Hey Ms. Vickey we ain't gonna have no problems witya kickin ass tonight"

"Well boys I aint gonna promise you nothin but these bitches betta not try to play me"

"Ms. Vickey you're to fine to be breakin shit up"

"Aight boys ya'll hava goodnight"

The double doors where opened and I walked through to the crowd looking for signs of Mike. The music was blazing and the crowded dance floor was full of folks strutting their stuff. I spotted the usual groupies as they circled around the players looking for a chance to get wit them. I walked over to the bar and ordered a glass of red wine. I looked across the floor to the VIP section and of course I noticed the usual people showing off their wealth. It was then I noticed Mike and Mya sitting together at a table talking by themselves. She leaned on him and brushed against his arm while they talked. I quickly walked through the crowd and headed over to his table interrupting his conversation with Mya.

"This is why you can't answer your phone" I said while standing over his table.

HEADGAME by Brandy

"Excuse me but we're talking" Mya said as she interrupted my stare down with Mike.

"Bitch you need to stay outta this before I kick your ass again" I moved around the table readying to commence to jumpin on this bitch. Mike must of recognize the seriousness of the situation and moved in between us.

"Come on Vickey you ain't gotta do that" He said

"Your right because your not worth it"

I rolled my neck and turned to walk away for him but Mike attempted to grab my arm. Once I felt his finger grasping my arm I pushed away from him. I accented my walk with a shake that made my ass jiggle. The pumps gave my ass more bounce as I moved gracefully toward the dance floor. I danced with the nearest guy I saw and enticingly wrapped my hands around his waist pressing against his body as I grinded my ass all over his manhood. I moved with his body as he wrapped his arms around me and pressed his dick against me. I could feel the result of my work as his stiffened dick poked at me. It wasn't three minutes into my dance that I felt Mike breathing on my neck and trying to get my attention.

"What are you doin?" Mike yelled as he grabbed my arm and interrupted my dancing.

"What it look like I'm doin?" I said as I swung my torso in a grinding motion between my partner's legs.

HEADGAME   by Brandy

"We need to talk right know Vickey" He started to direct me off the dance when my unknown dance partner tried to stop Mike from interrupting our dance.

"YO partna maybe da lady don't wanna go witya" My sudden dance partner intervene as he grabbed my hand pulling me away for Mike. Mike recognized the challenge he was given and swung the hardest Mike Tyson left hook he could muster. Mike's punch snapped his head back on impact and twisted his entire face around. His head jerk back and the force of the blow knocked him to the floor. Mike led me to the back of the club so we could have a private moment.

"You got some nerve Vickey , you comin pullin that bullshit"

"Fuck you Mike go back to your little bitch over there, is that why you can't fuckin call me"

"Fuck that bitch, I was tryin to be good to you but you disappearing and shit. What happened to you Vickey?

"Alright... I had to deliver some money to some people in Philly and they tried to kill me.. I didn't tellya because I ain't want you involved in my shit.. The only nigga I been trying to get wit is you but you wanna act like you all that."

"That' all you had to say Vickey, You know I don't like secrets."

HEADGAME   by Brandy

"I'm sorry Mike, how long your gonna hold a grudge against me"

"Wow the great Vickey apologizes"

"Shut up!"

"Oh you sorry, come here and show me how sorry you are"

I leaned in for a kiss and his tongue swam inside my mouth. That night I went back to his condo and I got the fuck of my life. I let him have this pussy anyway he liked it. He slammed it from the back, front and side ways. His fat dick pulsated while his hard body dripped sweat all over me. He drove his dick deep inside as he pinned my legs back. His dick felt so good as it penetrated my fat pussy. When we switch position I rode his dick like I was riding a horse for the Wild West. I was so excited that my pussy exploded and my juices showered all over his dick. When he was nearing ejaculation his eye rolled back. I could feel his hot cum running down my legs as his body quivered and rested on top of mine.

Mike and I were tighter than ever. I could tell that good things were going to happen between us. It wasn't long before I moved in with him at his upstate New York ranch. I kept my room over at Jessie's because I spent the night there when Mike's team was playing out of town. I was happy that Mike's football season was almost over in a couple of days. He was so excited that his team made it to the Super bowl but I didn't know it was

HEADGAME   *by Brandy*

such a big deal. He says that why he likes me because I'm wasn't a football groupie. Every body seemed to keep talking about this big game called the super bowl but I don't see the big deal.

Jessie and I had become so close that I trusted her with everything I owned and knew. She was like the sister I never had. I was happy that she finally settled down with one player and remained loyal to him. Jessie explained the big deal of the stupid bowl and convinced me to go to Florida for the game. I didn't care to go to out of state games because I hated all the fuss of traveling. He continued beg and bribe me until I agreed to travel to Florida. I tried everything to get out of going to the stupid bowl but he was not having it.

"It is only the biggest game of my life and I want you there watching me," he'd say with those big brown eyes glaring at me. I was truly in love with Mike and it made me happy that we were together. Officially we've been together for about six months now and I must admit his sex was so good. It felt so good to me that I rolled over and cried. I was embarrassed to show my feelings for him but as time pasted I was able to declare my love with out remorse. I only wanted be around him because he was kind and generous to me. Mike loved giving me gifts and taking me on shopping trips. The truth was Mike promised me another expensive shopping trip if I attended the Super bowl in Orlando Florida.

HEADGAME by Brandy

Jessie and I arrived in Florida that Saturday, a day before the scheduled big game. The arriving airport was over crowded as the masses gathered to witness the Champions from each division to play. They would battle to win this last game of the season and be crowned the Super bowl world champions. The hotels were packed with visitors anxiously waiting for the game to start and giving into the hype of the challenge that lay before them. Mike was swarmed by reporters trying to get an interview with him. The sports fans swarmed the team players every time they walk out of their hotel rooms.

The day of the Super bowl was filled with hysteria as the football maniacs came to witness the carnage of bodies falling on the field. The traffic to the Stadium was so congested that it would take an hour to find parking. Jessie and I wore our special all access VIP passes that allowed us to walk the entire stadium. A private party box was rented for our entertainment and leisure. We invited the famous R&B singer from Hollywood to join us to watch the game. His entourage was a mellow crowd of people and they handled themselves with class. Every since my run in with Terror Tee I stay away from the entertainment crowd. However he was cool and I loved his new music CD. I sat in the front row watching the game and sippin on cognac. I really wasn't watching the game closely and Jessie took notice in how bored I'd become. I only paid attention to the game when I saw Mike playing. I watched him move fast as he forcefully ran through the other team's defense. He seemed unstoppable as he dodged blockers and

HEADGAME				by Brandy

tacklers with his quick finesse moves. The crowd chanted wildly as I watched him run with the ball as he boldly charged toward the challenging team. A tackler grabbed him by the waist and dragged him to the ground. His helmet crashed into another player and his ankle twisted oddly. When the game play was over Mike was on the ground motionless. The EMS workers entered the playing field carrying a stretcher and a medical bag. I stood to my feet with both hands covering my face and praying he was alright. The crowd was buzzing with worried on lookers and for some reason I kept thinking of that Good times episode of when Keith hurt his leg. I kept thinking the worst possible scenario and that he may be crippled for the rest of his life. The thought of him being paralyzed frightened me so much. Jessie could see the horror in my face and held me close to her as we watch him lay on the ground still motionless. Mike finally picked himself off the ground and stumbled to the sidelines. The crowd began to cheer him and I was relieved to see him walking. It was like a breath of fresh air to see him moving around. I felt the relief watching him recover but I wondered how serious his injuries were. Jessie instinctively called down to the field to get a progress report on Mike's injuries.

"He's alright it looks like he sprained his ankle," Jess said comforting me in a soothing voice. It was almost time for the halftime show and the R&B Singer that shared the booth went to get prepared for his performance. We were alone and waiting for the half time show to start. I hurried to the bathroom so I could watch the start of the show. While doing my business I heard Jessie whispering

HEADGAME by Brandy

over the phone. When I opened the door and walked out of the bathroom she quickly hung up the phone. This made me suspicious and I curiously asked who she was talking to.

"Who was dat?" I asked.

"Nobody you know, just come here and watched the half time show," She said. I walked over to the seat and sat along side her to watch the much bragged about halftime show. The show started shortly after the introduction by the announcer and the lights coordinated with the sound system. The famous singer began his performance on the fifty yard line. He was soon joined in by a famous female singer. The singer's performance sent the crowd screaming into frenzy. The finale included a marching band coming on stage and encircling the singer. The fireworks exploded and lighting added drama to the ending of his performance. The crowd danced in the isle to the music, cheered and applauded until the show was over.

"Thank you! Thank you! Could all of you please take a look at the screen," The singer announced after he performed his act. I was looking away from the massive 200 foot television screen as it displayed my name.

V.I.C.K.E.Y   D.I.A.M.O.N.D the large fluorescent screen blinked, catching the crowds attention. My hands covered my face as I soon noticed the television cameras focusing their lens on me. I could not believe what was happening as I took cover into Jessie chest. The words flashing on the

HEADGAME   by Brandy

large screen surprised me as it did the entire world WILL YOU MARRY ME.... LUV MIKE the 200 foot colored screen read and I was so takin off guard that I didn't know what do. Jessie handed me the phone and it was Mike talking on the line.

"Vickey will take me as your husband?" He asked over the phone. I was shocked and surprise of his proposal.

"Yes," I shouted and shook my head in agreement with all the excitement I could muster. When the large television screen showed my reaction the stadium roared in pandemonium as they hollered and screamed at me.

"She said yes! She said yes! The crowded chanted over and over. My proposal was the most incredible moment of my life and I was grinning until the end of the game. When I came on the field Mike hugged me tightly and gave me a five carat diamond ring to seal the deal.

HEADGAME   *by Brandy*

The wedding

The wedding ceremony was to be performed by the famous a Reverend Marshall Walker he flew in from California. It was a beautiful afternoon for my wedding and I was excited to get all the attention. Mike's family drove down from Ohio to celebrate their son's nuptials. His mother presented me with

HEADGAME   by Brandy

a diamond broche that has been in their family since the 1880's. I already splurged on a diamond necklace, earrings that matched the large stone Mike gave me. The expensive diamonds glistened off my body as it sparkled in the light. I was being pampered and Mike layed the world at my feet. It was a gorgeous day and I was nervous as my bride's maid sat around drinking zippendales and talking a mile a minute. Jessie, Mike's sister and his cousin filled the bride's maid's position. Mike's father offered to walk me down the isle, to give me away. I wished my Dad was alive so he could see his little girl getting married to a star football player. I always thought when my wedding day came Khadija, Margi and Carmen would be by my side as brides maids. My wedding dress was the most beautiful dress that I ever seen. I remember the day when the designer took the measurements and promised that this was going to be the most extravagant she ever made. It was a spectacular white long flowing gown trimmed in ruffles, shear and studs that sparkled when the reflecting lights shined on it. Jessie was right beside me and taking care of all the details. She ensured that I wanted for nothing and all I ever needed was provided to me. I stared into three way mirror and I begun to emotionally cry. My tears expressed the love I was giving and receiving. I was so used to being for myself and until this point I only relied on me but know I finally had an unselfish love of my own. Jessie quickly cradled me in her arms with the reassurance that everything would go perfect and I had nothing to worry about.

HEADGAME   *by Brandy*

" I'm so emotional because I can't believe that I deserve all these good things in my life, I've done some horrible things in the past" I said.

"You deserve to be happy and to have a good life"

"You really believe that"

"Yes I do"

I felt as if I was the luckiest women in the world. I finally achieved all my heart's desires, husband, love, house, money and cars. What more could I have asked for except giving birth to twins. I sent for my mother and had to hire a nurse to care for her which recommended that she be sedated. I needed her presence even though I wasn't sure if she knew what was going on.

 Saint Johns cathedral was rented for this occasion and the custom embroidered announcements were mailed to our guest months earlier. The massive and marbled Cathedral was built over two hundred years ago, it was decorated with large stained glass window. The red carpet streamed out to the elevated pulpit and the mahogany wooden pews held up to 300 guest. It was a twenty minute drive from the house to the Cathedral and I needed to be on time. The house was filled with guest as they prepared for the wedding ceremony. The tent company was fixing and prepping for the reception in the back yard. The doubled parked delivery trucks crowded the street as the caterer's unloaded pounds of food.

HEADGAME   by Brandy

I wanted to look my best so I hired the best designer to make my dress. I intentionally told the designer to make it a size smaller so I had to diet and lose 10 pounds to fit into my dress. The society papers where jockeying for the first look of the gal who stole this athlete's heart. His proposal while at the Super bowl made a celebrity of my own.

I starved myself because I could not eat my favorite junk foods especially chili cheese nachos with extra chili. I loved my fatty foods and I couldn't live with out them. Jessie coached me on how to do walk gracefully down the steps so I wouldn't fall. I'd practiced in those high heels until my feet were pounding. I had to hide my Philly swagger and put on my best deinty princess act.

I was flattered when the make up artist arrived to make me beautiful. He covered my face with foundation hiding all the small scars I acquired throughout my journey. My eyebrows were arched and the peach covered lipstick made my lips look so sexy. Lastly the tiara was place a top of my head crowning me like a new princess. I was stunning and ready to go meet with my new husband. A box was delivered to the house and it was a dozen of red roses. I picked up the card and read it, *Best Wishes Love Jamal Jr.* I could hardly swallow as I curiously wondered how he knew that I was getting married today. How he was able to locate me was cause to call off the wedding. If he knew I was here than who else can find me so easily.

HEADGAME   *by Brandy*

"You look so beautiful Vickey they're waiting for you...Is something wrong?," Jessie asked. I hesitated before I answered her and I choose to ignore the flowers. I made believe that nothing was wrong as I hide my deepest fears. The wedding would go on as planned.

I slowly walked to the stairs readying my pose for the photographers. I counted 45 seconds and began to make my descent elegantly moving from one step to another. When I got midway I hit a pose allowing the photographers another moment to snap shots of me. I finally reached the bottom step and gracefully walked to the door. The standing, starting and the posing went on until I reached the limousine. I looked inside it was filled with Jessie, my mother and some of his relatives that I never seen. I turned around for one more picture and waved to the camera. BOOM! A bomb was detonated sending shrapnel and fire throw the car killing all inside............

If you want a sneak preview of Volume 2 hit me up on face book:

HEADGAME — by Brandy
Search: **beesunshyne@yahoo.com**

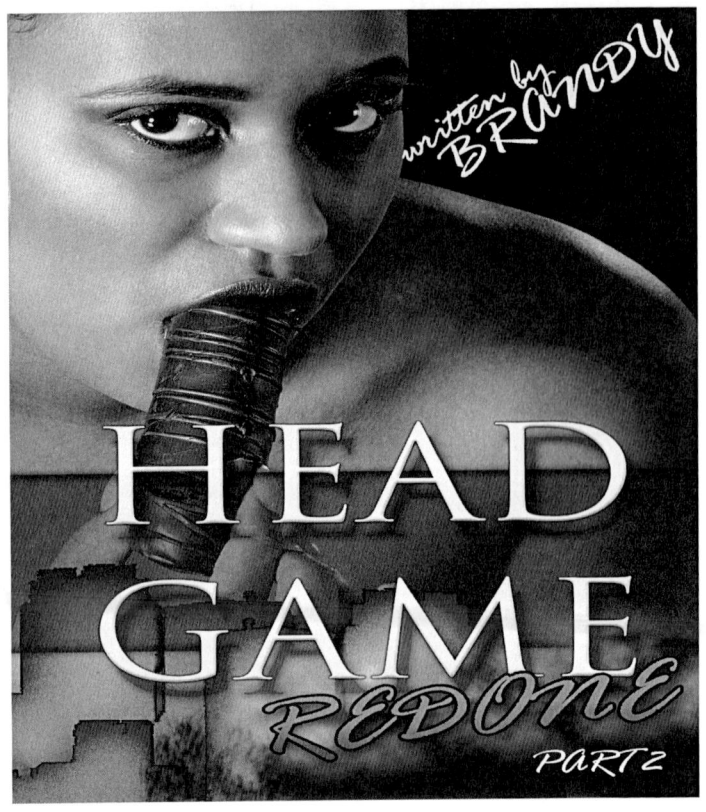